The Survivors' Walk

A Novel

The Survivors' Walk

A Novel

Jackie Ryan Witherspoon

For Gina —
Stay Strong —
We rock!
Love, Jackie

Two Harbors Press
322 First Avenue N, 5th floor
Minneapolis, MN 55401
612.455.2293
www.TwoHarborsPress.com

ISBN-13: 978-1-63413-794-2
LCCN: 2015915427

Distributed by Itasca Books

Cover Design by Biz Cook
Typeset by JAAD Book Design

Printed in the United States of America

For Mary

Contents

Chapter 1

Jessie Gifford sat at the antique round oak table in her kitchen, her cell phone lodged between her ear and shoulder, and traced the curlicues in the wood grain with her index finger, wishing she had never answered the phone.

Instinctively, she'd known that Dr. Ames calling after office hours probably didn't signal good news. After seeing the familiar number on caller ID, she had answered the phone cheerfully, hoping her happy tone would impact whatever he had to tell her. Make the news good. Or stall him, at least, if it wasn't.

In the two days since he'd ordered a second mammogram, this one labeled "diagnostic," she had almost forgotten that she was waiting to hear test results. She'd had unclear results from mammograms and Pap tests before, and follow-up exams then had shown everything was fine. Just fine.

Throughout the ordeal of these tests, she'd harbored a nagging thought that maybe, this time, something was wrong, truly wrong, but she hadn't allowed the idea to settle into her mind. It would be okay. It always had been.

She continued to follow the lines and loops of the wood with her finger as she listened to the voice on her cell phone, thinking she should really pull the table apart and clean out the center brace where crumbs liked to gather. And she hadn't even started fixing supper. What did she have on hand?

Gradually, the doctor's words began to sink in. The results were back. He didn't like what he saw. They wouldn't know much more until she had an MRI and then a biopsy. He would be happy to make the arrangements in the morning for her to see a specialist to get all of that rolling.

Jessie realized the phone had gone silent, the doctor waiting for her to say something.

"I feel like we're talking about someone else." Her voice was barely a whisper. "I feel like I should say, 'How is she doing?' but it's me we're talking about."

The doctor's reply was equally quiet, as if he was struggling to find the right words. And couldn't. "I know. These calls are so hard to make," he said. "You've had the rug pulled out from under you. Talk to Greg. Try not to worry too much. We'll take this one step at a time."

From what seemed like a great distance away, in some sort of hazy spot, Jessie saw that her husband had walked in from work during the call. She later wondered how Greg knew immediately that something was wrong. She didn't remember answering the doctor or even finishing the phone call. She was just suddenly standing, shaky and unable to take a step, fear freezing her in place.

Maybe he thinks someone has died, she thought and tried to smile to let him know that wasn't the case.

Amazingly, or maybe from habit perfected over twenty-eight years of marriage, when one was shaken, the other became stronger. Jessie walked to Greg and wrapped her arms around his waist, resting her face against his chest.

"Who was on the phone?" Greg asked, sounding angry, but Jessie knew that wasn't the case. He was scared.

"Dr. Ames. It seems my routine mammogram wasn't so routine," she said and then quickly added, "It's probably nothing."

Not much more was said between them that night about the phone call. What was there to say? All they knew as absolute fact was that something might be wrong. Maybe everything was fine. Or maybe she was in for the fight of her life. For her life. Thoughts tumbled through Jessie's mind, tangling with a fear that made her sick to her stomach. She felt like someone had died. Her mind was fuzzy, her body suddenly unfamiliar. She wasn't sure how to act. She was furious with Dr. Ames. How dare he scare her like this! She had been going to him all of her adult life. He knew her body inside and out, literally. He was probably being overly cautious and, in the process, scaring them half to death.

Jessie tried to put the phone call and Dr. Ames's words out of her mind. She and Greg watched a murder mystery on television, laughed together, and made comments on the show's advertisements. It was a game between them to find a connection of why certain companies and products would support specific television programs.

"Ah. Car insurance. Makes sense," Greg said, feigning understanding. "If she had only purchased good car insurance, she could have gotten away from the killer. Driven faster, knowing her car was well insured."

Jessie laughed, and it felt good. Almost normal. When the next commercial came on, she joined in the banter. "Deodorant. For feminine hygiene yet. Oh, yeah. Very important any time you are dealing with a murderer."

Greg laughed louder than the joke warranted and moved his hand to cover hers where it rested between them, giving her fingers a tender squeeze. The care between them now was so fragile, the fear so strong. Jessie wiped away unexpected tears before Greg could see. Both of them were trying to keep the tone between them as light as possible. They clung to life as they had known it only hours earlier, treasuring the quiet evening watching television and not wanting to look ahead.

Jessie told Greg everything that the doctor had said: he would schedule a biopsy and an MRI, make an appointment for her with a breast specialist, and they would know more after that. She should try to stay positive and not worry.

Greg assured her that he'd go with her to all of the appointments and that everything would be okay. But she knew neither one of them was sure of that.

After they had gone to bed, and she was positive Greg was asleep from the sound of his breathing, Jessie slipped from under the covers. After grabbing her coat from the hall stand, she stood alone on their back deck in the dark, feeling numb, and looked up to the sky filled with pinpricks of sparkling stars.

She looked for the three stars in a line that were her private anchor.

The stars were there. They had to be. If she had ever needed them, it was now.

Jessie knew her friends and family shook their heads in resigned acceptance of her superstitious nature. She always made a wish when the clasp on a necklace met the charm; she never passed a salt shaker from hand to hand; and she certainly never walked under ladders.

No one knew, however, that she had three stars as good-luck charms. That was part of the bargain; she couldn't tell anyone about them, or the good luck they promised wouldn't work.

From some contact with astrology in her past, she thought she remembered that the bright stars made up the belt of a constellation warrior from Greek mythology. To Jessie, they were simply a comfort.

If the stars did indeed belong to a warrior, even better. She could use a fighter on her side just now. And luck.

The sky was beginning to turn pink and orange at the horizon. The birds were beginning to rouse, but there was no traffic yet. Jessie thought of the children who lived on her street, still warm in their beds, and she felt a sudden and surprising envy.

The January day promised to be cold and clear. She shivered and pulled her heavy coat more tightly around her. Her eyes felt gritty as she looked for her stars. With the sun starting to rise, she had to find them soon before they disappeared into a sunny sky. She felt a sense of panic but then smiled as she saw them, her three stars in a row. She wasn't praying, really, and if she was honest, she didn't actually believe the stars would bring her luck. It was more like she was trying to grab hold of some sense of reality. Even when clouds blocked them from sight, Jessie knew the stars were always there. Right now, it seemed they were the only constant in life.

Jessie turned from the sight of her stars, pushed open the sliding door, and was hanging her coat back up when Greg walked into the kitchen, wiping sleep from his eyes.

"Going somewhere?" he asked, nodding toward the coat in her hands. "You know you still have on your pajamas, right?"

Jessie smiled. "Yes, I'm aware of that. I just needed some air."

Greg didn't know about her stars, and for a second, Jessie thought about sharing that part of her life with him but didn't. The stars were hers alone. She was afraid he'd make a joke about them if she told him, tell her it was crazy to think the stars were her personal good-luck charms. He'd come up with some sort of platitude to start the day, and she didn't need his persistently positive attitude this morning. She didn't want cheering up. She didn't want a pep talk. She didn't feel like laughing.

She felt detached from herself; that's how she felt. She was watching another woman from a distance. She wasn't prepared for this. She was the person who could always bounce back from whatever life threw at her, but this was a solid and unfamiliar punch to the gut.

She knew people—acquaintances, friends, even family members—who had died from serious illnesses, but she'd never before given much thought, if any, to the day they had received the diagnosis. Had they too wondered if the doctor had made a mistake? If it was all a bad dream? Had they been afraid, like she was?

She understood now how life could be great one day and something you might not survive the next.

It surprised Jessie, as she spooned coffee into the filter and turned on the pot, that her thoughts this morning weren't of her children, her husband, or her family at all. Instead she thought about all of the things in life she'd planned to experience and now might not.

She had always wanted to travel. With the kids now on their own, she had started looking online for deals on trips to Europe, Mexico, or maybe New Zealand. She was sure she could convince Greg to take a trip, once she settled on a destination.

She had thought she might go back to school, earn her master's degree, and possibly teach.

They had talked about looking for a vacation home, maybe on a lake somewhere, a getaway for the two of them, where the kids and their families—when they had families—could join them.

Knowing she was being overly dramatic but not caring that she was, Jessie allowed the depression in. There was a possibility, maybe a good possibility, that none of those things would happen.

She dreaded the start of the day and the expected phone call from Dr. Ames to "get the ball rolling." She hoped Greg would go into work. It was going to be hard enough to wait for the call without listening to him pace the house.

But he stayed in his boxers as she poured them each a cup of coffee, and he sat down in the recliner as if he wasn't sure what role he should play.

"Aren't you going to work?" Jessie asked, hoping he couldn't hear the panic she was beginning to feel. She didn't understand it herself. Nothing in life had changed. Her family doctor just wanted her to have a more complete checkup. No big deal. She certainly didn't need her husband making it so. Or hovering over her all morning. Or being overly concerned. Or overly cheerful, which was more likely.

Greg looked up at her, holding the remote control to the TV, as if seeking permission to turn it on.

"I'd really rather you go to work," Jessie said. "I have work to do, too. Seriously, go. I can let you know when Dr. Ames calls. If he calls."

The phone call was only to set up appointments with other doctors, Jessie told herself again. And that might take a while. Besides, the specialists would likely tell them that everything was fine, that the tests done at the local hospital were wrong. That this had all been some kind of a mistake. She felt a moment of tenderness for Dr. Ames. He would be so sorry that he had worried them.

Chapter 2

On the other side of town, in one of the new subdivisions that seemed to be forever popping up, Marcie Tomson looked at the stacks of boxes that surrounded her. She'd been so eager to move into their new home that she had forgotten how daunting the task was of unpacking all of their belongings and finding new places for everything. She should have remembered; this was their fourth move in seven years.

Absentmindedly, she smoothed her hand over the small bump at the top of her breast she had discovered this morning in the shower. It wasn't painful, but now that she knew it was there, she didn't seem to be able to stop rubbing it, and that did make it hurt.

Yesterday she'd helped the movers bring in any boxes that she could carry, even with their protests that she was doing their job. She had just wanted the job done and them gone. Anything she could do to speed that along she'd been willing to do. She'd probably just pulled a muscle or something. Still, the bump was a little worrisome.

Now, after her first shower in their new home and surrounded by moving boxes, she wasn't sure where to start.

Marc, her husband, hadn't had any such problem. He'd set up the desk first and then plugged in the computer and had made sure everything was up and running before he left to drop the kids off at school and daycare before going to work.

Unpacking the boxes marked for each child's room, the kitchen, the bathrooms, and every other room would be up to her. The movers had put the boxes in the appropriate rooms, and the kids' rooms would probably be easiest, but she moved toward the kitchen. Once the dishes, glassware, and pots and pans were put away, she'd feel more like she was really home.

Still, the small bump located just at the top of her right breast stayed on her mind. It was probably nothing. She wasn't as careful with her breasts as she supposed a woman should be, actually using them for leverage as she hefted boxes into the house. *Leverage might be a stretch*, she thought, smiling to herself. She didn't have much in the breast department. Probably not as much as Marc would have liked, but she was happy with her size.

Rubbing her palm against the bump again, she found herself sitting at the computer and typing "breast lumps" into the browser. It wouldn't hurt anything to see what it said on the various sites devoted to the subject. She just needed to alleviate her fears.

Two hours later, she had learned that the majority of lumps aren't anything to worry about, especially for women under the age of forty with no history of cancer in the family. She smiled to herself. She was thirty-four. So far, so good. She continued to check websites devoted to the subject of breast lumps, with information accompanied by photographs, drawings, and graphs. The sheer number of sites was alarming.

In a chat room—not the most reliable of sources but still a source—she read that if the lump was painful, it probably wasn't anything. That's what one woman said, anyway.

Deciding to put the theory to the test, Marcie consciously tried to stop rubbing the area while she began pulling items out of boxes. She didn't know if the lump hurt or not. She'd made it hurt by constantly checking it. She couldn't tell if it was "moveable" or not—one site had mentioned that aspect to lumps. She pulled up the website again. She couldn't remember if a lump that was moveable was good or bad.

The doorbell chimed, making her jump, but she was happy for the interruption. Smiling, she headed for the front door, relatively sure who it would be. Although she and Marc had changed houses, they'd remained in the same neighborhood, and she was surprised it had taken her friends this long to come over.

"All unpacked and ready for company?" Lisa, her best friend, pushed open the front door and stepped over boxes still stacked in the foyer. "Let me guess. You started in the kids' rooms. You're such a mom."

Marcie laughed. "Oh, you think you know me so well. I'll have you know I started in the kitchen. And the coffee's on."

"Your coffee is always on. That's why I love you." Lisa led the way toward the spacious kitchen, noting her approval. The kitchen had been one of the plusses for the house. It was bright and sunny with sliding glass doors that looked out to the backyard, now covered with a fine layer of frost.

"Looks homey already," Lisa said. She reached for a cup from the shelf, filled it, and then refilled Marcie's as well. "What's next? I'm at your service."

"Kids' rooms, I guess," Marcie said, and both laughed at her predictability. "Well, seriously. I want them done before they get home from school. Maybe their rooms will stay neat for a couple of hours at least."

Lisa cocked her head, looking quizzically at her friend. "You seem kind of distracted. The house is fabulous. You love it, don't you? I'd give anything for all of your space."

"I do love it." Marcie grinned, unaware that she was again rubbing the spot on her chest.

Lisa looked down at her friend's hand and then back to her face. "Did you get hurt? I told you to leave it all to the movers, but you had to help, didn't you?"

"Just a few boxes. They were taking forever."

"And now something hurts?"

"Just a little bump. I noticed it in the shower this morning. Probably pulled a muscle or something."

Lisa stood up from where she had been sitting on a bar stool and moved closer to her friend. "Let me see."

Ordinarily, Marcie would have argued. Good grief, their friendship didn't extend to showing each other every bump and bruise, and she was surprised at herself when she pulled her T-shirt low enough to expose the now-tender spot at the top of her breast.

The doorbell rang again, followed by the sound of the door opening. Both women turned as one to see who had entered. Emily, the third friend to make up their trio, walked into the kitchen, carrying a pan of cinnamon rolls.

"Okay, they're from a can, but . . ." Emily said, before noticing Marcie and Lisa looking serious, with Marcie's T-shirt pulled down from one shoulder. "What's going on? New house *and* new lingerie? That ought to get Marc's attention."

The edge in her voice wasn't lost on Marcie. Emily had never liked Marc and was barely able to hide the fact. Marc didn't even try to disguise his disapproval of Emily. The tension between them was a mystery to Marcie. She loved them both.

The three women tried to laugh, but the mood in the room had shifted to a somber tone.

"Marcie found a lump in the shower this morning," Lisa said, her voice quiet.Laughing, Marcie moved away from the counter and grabbed a cup for Emily, filling it with coffee and then making a production of lifting the foil from the plate of rolls. "It's nothing. Lord, Lisa. You're so dramatic." She smiled at Emily. "I helped the movers bring in some boxes last night and just pulled a muscle. That's all." Seeing the serious look on her friends' faces had Marcie laughing more. "You guys have been watching too much TV. It's nothing. Believe me. I'm thirty-four years old. I don't have a lump."

Lisa refused to let the subject rest. "Did you tell Marc?"

Marcie shook her head. "Of course not. I'm telling you it's a pulled muscle. It'll probably be gone by tomorrow. Are you guys here to help or not?"

She was happy to see her friends and glad they were sharing this moment of settling into a new home, but their drama was becoming irritating. The lump was nothing.

According to what she'd read on the websites, it wasn't even really a lump. The skin just felt a little thicker there. That was all. Good grief.

Sensing Marcie's growing irritation, Lisa and Emily let the subject drop and followed their friend upstairs to the bedrooms.

"Which room first?" Emily asked.

The atmosphere lighter, Marcie led them into a bedroom painted pale pink, with frilly eyelet curtains on the windows. "This is Ellie and Madi's room. Ellie will want to see her stuffed animals and Barbies out when she gets home. Let's do it first—if you're really here to help, that is."

"Absolutely," Lisa and Emily said in near unison, and all three laughed.

By lunchtime, the rooms for Marcie and Marc's three children—Ellie, seven; Christopher, five; and Madi, three—were empty of boxes. Their clothes were in their respective dressers and closets, favorite toys lined the window sills, and the laundry baskets Marcie had been trying to teach all three to use were placed in the corner of each room.

She and Marc's room could wait, Marcie decided. The cinnamon rolls were calling, and the three friends trooped back to the kitchen to grab forks and plates and to reheat the coffee in their cups.

Seated once more at the center island, Marcie groaned as she took a bite of her roll, waving her fork at her two friends. "Canned or not, these are fabulous. Thanks, Emily. I needed this. I'll have to walk an extra mile to work it off, but it's worth it."

Lisa chewed on her own roll, scraping the extra topping off the side of the plate with her finger and letting it melt in her mouth, all the while eyeing Marcie. “Okay, I know this is going to piss you off, but let’s have a look. Seriously.”

She didn’t have to explain what she meant. Marcie knew that as they’d been pulling toys and dolls from boxes, making up the beds, and putting clothes into dressers that the subject of her “lump” would be brought up again.

Rather than fight what she was fairly sure would be a losing battle, Marcie stretched her T-shirt down again until the area in question could be seen. Lisa and Emily both moved closer.

Lisa cautiously rubbed her finger over the raised spot. “Does it hurt?” she asked, looking up to lock eyes with Marcie.

“No,” Marcie answered. “Well, at least I don’t think it does. I haven’t been able to leave it alone since I found it, so I don’t know if it really hurts or if I’m just making it hurt.”

“I don’t think it’s anything,” Emily said. “I really don’t. It doesn’t look like what I’ve always thought a lump would look like.”

Lisa leaned back on the bar stool. “And you’re saying that because of your extensive medical training?”

Marcie laughed, wanting to lighten the mood between her two friends. “Well, I have to admit that I looked up breast lumps on the Internet. I don’t think this looks anything like what the pictures showed, either. It’s not even in my breast. Just at the very top.”

"Have it checked out anyway," Lisa said. "You're probably right. It's probably nothing, but you'll feel better if a doctor tells you that. Seriously. And so will we."

Marcie knew they were right. She truly didn't think it was anything, but she would feel better knowing that. She promised both of her friends that she'd call the doctor for an appointment the minute they left, but after they did, she put their plates, cups, and forks in the new dishwasher and decided to set up the laundry room. That would be a quick task; plus, the room would need to be ready for use tonight.

And she didn't forget about making the appointment. She really didn't. She just put it off. It could wait.

Chapter 3

Jessie stood in front of the bathroom mirror, staring at her reflection, trying to decide if she looked different. She felt different—that was for sure. People usually guessed her to be younger than forty-eight. She kept her hair highlighted, styled in chunky layers, and typically tucked behind her ears. She walked daily and ran at least three times a week to keep her figure slim. She enjoyed going out with girlfriends at least once a month to have a few drinks and laughs and to share the joys and trials of husbands, marriage, kids, jobs, and life in general.

She enjoyed her work as a freelance journalist and the freedom it allowed her. The money wasn't as good as it had been when she'd been on the staff of the daily newspaper, but she liked being able to choose her own articles to write. The trade-off was worth it.

The kids were quickly becoming grown-ups. All three were doing well and, as far as she knew, were happy. Greg enjoyed his work and found time now for golf and fishing. Yes, money was still tight, but time was more valuable. Life was good.

And now this. She didn't relish the idea of sharing *this*. Not with anyone. If she did appear different this morning, she'd earned it after a night of tossing and turning as she tried to put the phone call into perspective. Greg, finally, had decided to go into work, and Jessie eyed the unmade bed with longing, wishing she could climb back in and pull the covers over her head. She wanted to stay there all day. She didn't know what the day would bring. Should she tell people what was going on? Friends? Family? How would she tell their three kids? Her sister? Her brother? Her mom? They were going about their own lives just fine, and she was about to drop a bomb on them.

It felt that way, anyway. She didn't know what further tests would show. Maybe nothing. Probably nothing. It was the not knowing that was scary. She decided to wait to tell the kids and her family what was going on when she knew what was going on.

She felt the same, physically at least, as she had just one day before, but life felt very different. The future wasn't a sure thing, which was a thought she'd never had.

Greg was wonderful, right from that phone call in the kitchen, although Jessie's feelings alternated between anger at him for what she perceived as a lack of concern to anger at him for being too caring, too sympathetic. He had given her a lingering, tender hug before leaving for work, but even that had been irritating. Typically, he gave her a quick peck on the cheek and was out the door. Basically, Jessie realized, she was just angry. Period. At everyone. That's how she was reacting to this news that she might have cancer. She didn't have to wonder anymore about how she would handle it. She was angry, and she didn't seem to be able to stop being angry.

The fear had already changed her, she realized. She didn't know who she would be at the end of this journey, but it already felt as if a big chuck of her identity had disappeared with the doctor's first phone call. She'd never been a worrier, but now she couldn't stop worrying.

More of her had fallen away with Dr. Ames's second call this morning. He had ordered a rushed MRI to be performed at 11:00 a.m., followed by an appointment with a breast surgeon, who would perform a biopsy. Jessie felt as if her body had turned against her.

Not wanting to stare into the frightened eyes in the mirror a moment longer, Jessie returned to the kitchen and called Greg, telling him about the appointments. She felt guilty for urging him to go to work, only to ask him to come back home a few hours later.

Greg waited in the hospital cafeteria during the MRI and then drove Jessie to see Dr. Susan Catterson, the specialist Dr. Ames had recommended. Arriving early for the appointment, they waited in Greg's truck in the parking lot. Jessie cried and quietly blew her nose. She kept telling herself the tears were just because she was scared, not because she expected bad news. She truly didn't. Greg, sitting sideways in his seat, kept his hand on the back of her neck. His own eyes were bright and shiny.

For Jessie, it seemed that control of her life had been snatched away in a matter of hours. She longed to go back in time. She wanted her only concern to be dinner plans and what she needed to pick up at the market. She wanted to ponder over what she was going to wear to her niece's wedding. She wanted to think about her work and the next article she would write. She wanted herself back.

The specialist's office was in a low red-brick building with a glassed front. Jessie and Greg walked toward it silently, holding hands. Signs in the parking lot pointed toward other buildings in the complex for specialists in other medical fields. People, in single file or in groups, went in and out of the different buildings, most walking quickly in the cold January air. It reminded Jessie of an ant farm—everyone busy and everyone with a task to accomplish, like it or not. And it appeared that for some of the people, those bent over and walking against the wind, the burden was almost heavier than their bodies were capable of carrying.

Greg stayed in the visitors' lounge, at Jessie's request, while the biopsy was done in a dimly lit room, just large enough for the doctor and her nurse. They had warned her that it would be a little painful, but the truth was it hurt like hell, and she cried through the entire thing, both from pain and fear.

Afterward, Dr. Catterson's nurse summoned Greg from the waiting area to join them in the exam room.

"You okay?" Greg mouthed to Jessie as he entered. He sat down in a plastic chair beside her and reached for her hand.

Jessie nodded but found she was irritated by his concern. Why was everyone acting so melodramatic? Good grief.

Everything was fine. She knew it was. It always had been. All of this had been unnecessary and ridiculous.

Dr. Catterson sat on a rolling, armless stool in front of them, lightly touching Jessie's knee, glancing back and forth between her and Greg. "The biopsy will give us a lot more information," she said, "but after reviewing the results of the MRI, I expect it to confirm my belief that the mass is malignant."

Jessie heard the doctor's words through a heavy fog. She watched the woman's mouth making word shapes, but none of it made sense. Maybe she wasn't talking to her at all. The doctor was young and cute. She wore dark-gray tights covered by a long tunic of a soft mauve material that fell to just above her knees. Jessie kept her head down and stared at the doctor's shoes. Lace-up. Soft, gray leather. They looked comfortable. And expensive. *Would it be inappropriate to ask where she bought them?* she wondered. *Probably.*

"The MRI did show another tumor in the left breast," Dr. Catterson was saying. "We'll want another biopsy for that area. And we'll want to be aggressive with treatment. I strongly recommend a mastectomy, followed by chemotherapy and possibly radiation. We can talk with a plastic surgeon about reconstruction."

Jessie felt Greg's fingers tighten on her own. She heard the words from a distance: another mass. The other breast. Mastectomy. Radiation. Chemotherapy. Reconstruction.

Had Dr. Catterson asked a question? Jessie felt the blood rushing from her head, and she fought the sudden, overwhelming need to run from this room. She didn't want to sit in this chair, listening to these words she didn't understand, words that weren't part of her vocabulary.

She had just been told she had breast cancer. Dr. Catterson had used the word "malignant," but that was only semantics. The word "cancer" hung in the air like a bad smell they were all trying to ignore.

So much for her false tests in the past. So much for her belief that Dr. Ames had been wrong. So much for lucky stars.

This wasn't happening. This *couldn't* be happening. The feeling of watching another woman from a distance returned, and Jessie was curious about how the woman would react to the reality that, indeed, she did have breast cancer. And not just in one breast. In both of them. Probably.

Amazingly, when she did speak, Jessie's voice sounded strong. "Mastectomy. I want to go through this once and do whatever I have to do so it doesn't come back," she said, looking at Greg, willing him to say something—anything—that would make this all go away. He only nodded.

"Okay." Dr. Catterson pushed back on the stool, stood up, and then reached down and squeezed Jessie's and Greg's joined hands. With a promise that her nurse would call in a few days with more information and a surgery date, she smiled weakly at both of them and left the room.

Now it was real. Until only hours ago, hope had still existed that all of this had been a mistake—the tests were wrong. False alarm. No harm done.

It felt as if life was spiraling downhill at a speed Jessie couldn't stop.

She and Greg stood and followed Dr. Catterson out of the room and down a quiet hallway. Jessie purposefully held her head high, not allowing herself to give in to the fear that was lapping at the edges of her mind. She avoided eye contact with the other women in the waiting room, women waiting to hear their own fates. She didn't want to see their fear mirrored in her own eyes. She didn't want to belong to this club.

Chapter 4

From where she sat alone in a far corner of the waiting room, an unopened magazine on her lap, Irene Colstrum watched a woman walk down the hall. The woman looked shell-shocked. Obviously, the news she'd just received from Dr. Catterson hadn't been good. Irene knew that look. She'd seen in on the faces of other women she had watched come down that same hallway, through that same waiting room. It was the eyes. There was so much hurt and fear in them.

Irene's own eyes had probably looked the same the first time she'd made that walk. That all seemed so long ago but was only a few months, she realized. She'd trade places with this woman if she could, not out of any sense of altruism but of selfishness. The woman had what looked like a good man, likely her husband, by her side—something Irene had forgone when she'd opted to stay single, thinking a career was all she needed for fulfillment.

She regretted that decision now. Not always, just now.

And the woman was young—by comparison anyway. Irene smiled. The woman looked to be in her late thirties or early forties, cute, stylish. Had Irene been like her once? Maybe a million years ago. Irene probably had a good twenty or thirty years on the other woman.

I hope she'll be okay, Irene thought.

Chapter 5

After two weeks in the new house, it felt like home. *As it should*, Marcie thought. They'd only moved a couple of blocks down the street, but for Marc, it was moving *up* that mattered. The new house was pretentious in Marcie's mind, but for her husband, it was an outward sign that he was doing well.

And it was nice to have more space. She hoped they'd stay here for a while. The house was bigger than they needed, but the kids were growing up. Ellie wouldn't want to share a bedroom with her little sister forever, and Christopher's ever-growing collection of sports equipment would quickly consume his space.

Marcie had wandered into the laundry room, knowing there were clothes in the dryer that were ready to be folded, when the phone rang.

She walked back to the kitchen, sensing who was calling. Emily and Lisa had been asking her relentlessly if she'd made a doctor's appointment. She hadn't. Maybe today.

She didn't know why she was putting it off. Well, actually she did. Fear. The little lump at the top of her right breast hadn't disappeared as she'd hoped it would. *A bruise or a pulled muscle would have healed by now*, she thought. So what was this?

She'd spent more time on the Internet, trying to educate herself about breast lumps and what she should be looking for, and she'd done self-examinations in the shower every morning, something she'd never done before now.

She was thirty-four. Did women her age even get breast cancer? She knew the answer to that from the websites she had browsed. The answer was yes—but there wasn't any history of it in her family. So it was unlikely, right? Unlikely, but certainly possible.

The phone stopped ringing, but she knew it was only a matter of time before one or both of her best friends would be knocking on the door, asking again and for the hundredth time if she'd called the doctor.

Marc didn't act worried. She had finally summoned up the courage to tell him about the bump, but he hadn't seemed interested or concerned. She didn't know what was wrong between them, but something was. The closeness they'd known in the early years of their marriage was dissipating. That was normal, right? The kids had taken center stage, as they should.

Still, she wished she could talk to Marc about her fear that something might be seriously wrong.

Maybe it was just a pulled muscle, and it would take longer than a couple of weeks to heal. Maybe she had a hernia. Could you get those anywhere? She made a mental note to look that up.

The sound of the doorbell broke her thoughts and despite knowing what was about to come, she smiled. Her friends were nothing if not dependable.

With Emily and Lisa standing by her side, close enough to hear the conversation through the phone, she made the appointment with her family doctor, almost apologetic for wanting to have a "little bump" she had found near her breast checked out.

The doctor's nurse knew Marcie well from the numerous trips she had made to the clinic for inoculations for the three kids, the occasional scraped knee, and frequent ear infections—all three kids seemed to be susceptible to those. The nurse scheduled Marcie to see the doctor that afternoon

Lisa and Emily had gone along and also accompanied Marcie for her first mammogram the following morning, anxiously sitting in the waiting room to hear all about it.

"We want all the gory details," Emily had said.

Marcie drew the line, however, at their insistence that they go with her for the hurriedly scheduled MRI.

"I've got this, seriously," Marcie said. "I'm starting to feel like a member of a girl band." They had all laughed, but Lisa conceded only when Marcie told them Marc was going to be with her for the MRI.

It wasn't true. Marc hadn't wanted to hear anything about the test and certainly hadn't wanted to see the lump that was the cause of all the worry and flurry of activity. True, she had downplayed it. "It's probably nothing, but I feel like I should have it checked out," she had told him the evening before.

He'd looked up at her from where he sat on the leather recliner, his ever-present tablet on his lap. He'd stopped typing long enough that Marcie held her breath, wondering what she would say if he insisted on going with her.

"Yeah, you might as well check it out," he had said, returning to whatever he was doing on the tablet. "We pay enough for health insurance."

Marcie stared at the back of his head. That was it? That was the extent of his concern for his wife? She told herself that he was likely a little embarrassed that she might have something wrong with her breast. *Maybe he thinks it's gross*, Marcie thought, *even though it's barely visible. Still, the doctors seem to think it might be something. And if that turns out to be the case, Marc will step up*. She hoped.

Lying in a ridiculous position on the MRI table, she wished she had taken her friends up on their offer to come with her. This was definitely something they'd want to hear about. Her naked breasts fit through an opening on the table, where she lay on her stomach. She'd never felt more exposed, although she was still in her jeans.

"I know this isn't fun," the young man behind the glass partition said, "but stay as still as you can, so we won't have to start over."

He suggested she fill her thoughts with some fun memory to help pass the time and to keep her from feeling claustrophobic.

Too late for that, Marcie thought. She felt imprisoned before the test had barely started. She worked to keep her mind occupied by making lists—something she was good at, although no one knew the extent to which she went. She often wondered if she might have attention deficit disorder or some other type of phobia that involved constant list making.

The cold in the room prompted her to think of hot summer days. She loved being in the sun. Where had she sunbathed during her life?

1. The yard at the house where she grew up
2. On the grass outside of her college dorm room
3. At the first apartment she had shared with girlfriends
4. At the pool
5. At several pools, actually
6. At Marc's and her first home
7. At their third home (The second hadn't had a pool.)

Not yet at the new house, but she was looking forward to summer there. The house had a nicer, larger pool than their old house. The kids were going to love it.

Anywhere else? She couldn't think of any place, and then the thought hit her that she shouldn't be sunbathing anyway. Never should have, and if she did have cancer, had she caused it herself by dousing herself with baby oil and lying in the sun for hours? At the hottest time of the day. For years. Every summer since she'd been a teenager.

Just as the thoughts were turning into panic, the technician announced through a hidden microphone that the test was over.

Thank God. She wanted out of this place.

The technician assured her that the results of the MRI would be forwarded to Dr. Catterson's office, and they would be in touch with her. He didn't tell her not to worry. Maybe he wasn't supposed to do that. Maybe he didn't even know how to read the results; he just administered the test, but Marcie didn't think that was true. If he did this every day, all day, he probably had some idea about what he was seeing on the screen behind the glass partition. She tried to read his attitude. Was he looking at her with concern? No, he wasn't. He wasn't looking at her at all. He left her to dress and only spoke to ask if she knew her way back to the hospital's exit. Yes, she did.

Back in her car, she felt a surprising need to call someone. Tell someone what she had just been through. She didn't want to talk to Emily or Lisa. Not yet. They would know immediately that she was alone. That Marc hadn't accompanied her to the exam.

She wondered where Marc was. At work? Probably. It was only about one thirty. He might still be at lunch. Maybe he had taken a client out to eat. She could call him. And say what?

"I knew you would make light of it, and I knew you wouldn't come with me. But I just had an MRI to see if I have breast cancer, and I wanted to tell somebody."

She wondered briefly what her husband would say to that. He'd probably downplay it. Make her feel ridiculous for even going to the doctor and childish for being scared.

What had happened to them? Had it always been this way, and she'd just now realized it? Had Marc ever really been there for her when she needed him?

Of course he had. He'd been by her side when each of their children was born, and he had been caring and loving, so proud to be a father.

But that had been about him. Had he been concerned about how she felt, if the labor had been difficult, or if she was okay? She couldn't remember. Honestly, she'd been so excited when each of the kids had been born that she hadn't paid all that much attention to Marc either. That was normal. Probably.

She knew, without her friends saying so, that they didn't think much of Marc as a husband. He was a great socializer, a great host. His clients, coworkers, their friends, neighbors—everyone—loved coming to their parties. Marc was charming and funny. And good-looking.

He was a good father. He was a good provider. He didn't beat her, for heaven's sake. So he was a little distracted right now. She shouldn't be complaining. The new, larger house also had a new, larger mortgage, and she suspected Marc was worried about that, even though he'd deny it. He was working longer hours now than he had before. "Entertaining more prospective clients," he always answered when she asked about his long days.

She'd thought of suggesting that she go back to work but knew he'd frown on that idea. It would reflect badly on him. But she missed having somewhere to go in the mornings. She missed having coworkers and topics of conversation outside of being a mom. And of whatever might be going on with her body.

She wished she had enough confidence in Marc's love to have asked him to come with her today. But she felt strong, knowing she'd survived today on her own. It was all going to be okay.

She drove home, smiling and singing along with the radio, putting thoughts of the MRI out of her mind, thinking of what she'd fix for supper. Spaghetti, most likely. She always had the ingredients for that on hand. Everyone liked it, and it was quick and easy to make.

She created a list in her mind for how the evening would go. Once they had finished eating and the kids had bathed and put on their pajamas, she'd ask Marc to put them to bed tonight. She wanted to take a leisurely hot bath and get her mind organized for telling Marc about the MRI.

This health scare had made her realize that although she was only thirty-four, life was passing by in a blur of kids' activities. She had to find a way to regain herself—and her marriage.

And if the test showed that something was wrong, that the bump she thought was simply a bruise was more than that, then what? Marc would surely be there for her then. He would have to be, wouldn't he?

But, she thought, *the lump is going to turn out to be nothing*.

Chapter 6

A nurse phoned Jessie three days after the shattering ap-pointment with Dr. Catterson.

"My niece is getting married April 14," Jessie said, looking at the calendar that was soon to become a constant companion, with dates highlighted in different colors for different doctor appointments. Activities and upcoming plans would be crossed off the schedule in black ink.

"A wedding is an important occasion, and life doesn't stop," the nurse said, sounding on the verge of cheerful. "How about scheduling your mastectomy for the following week?"

"That would be great," Jessie said. *Great?* So now it was great that she was going to have major breast surgery? *What a stupid response*, she thought. But what would have been the right one? She just wanted to get off the phone. She wanted to deal with this on her own.

After the nurse and Jessie both consulted their calendars, the surgery was set for April, three months from now. Jessie had hoped that having a firm surgery date would put her mind at ease. It didn't. She fought against the idea that the cancer had already spread, that it was in her brain now. Some details were so foggy in her mind.

She couldn't remember the drive home after having the MRI and the biopsy. Had they stopped anywhere? Eaten anything? Talked about anything? If so, the memories were gone. What else had she forgotten?

The following morning Jessie mentally worked to memorize the taste of salty sunflower seeds and the bite of a Diet Pepsi as she and Greg took their new Jeep to a nearby lake. She didn't want to miss life, not even the smallest of details.

"We need to have some fun," Greg had said, finally persuading her to go with him. All Jessie could think about was that there was something in her body that might be growing, and that it might very well kill her. It might be killing her right now, and she was doing nothing to stop it. She just wanted it out.

As they drove down the winding tree-lined road, a glimpse of blue water ahead, she turned to look at Greg.

"I want to move the surgery up," she said. Her announcement surprised them both and then immediately felt right. This diagnosis was always there, an uninvited and unwelcome traveler accompanying them wherever they went.

"I want this out of me," Jessie said, "as soon as possible."

She hoped she didn't sound as shaky as she felt. The tumor growing inside her was the only thing on her mind, blocking out any possible moments of normalcy. For a split second when she awoke every morning, she thought ahead to the day, but then the growth inside her took over. It became like a separate entity, stealing her life away, moment by moment. It was hated, and she wanted it dead. It was like being pregnant, only in a bad sense. Her body was a host, but the entity growing inside her now was an alien being, ugly and despised. She saw it as something pulsating and gross, rather than the small blob of pink matter that it likely was.

Greg never took his eyes from the road, but she saw his jaw tighten.

"Whatever you want to do," he said. "I don't blame you for wanting it over. I can understand that. I know you wanted to wait until after the wedding, but I'll bet you'll be just fine by then anyway. I know it's important to you."

Jessie knew he didn't know what else to say, how to respond, how to lend her strength. She had always been a determined and independent person, or at least that was how she saw herself. Superstitions aside. Now, she wished someone, maybe Greg, would just take over. Make decisions for her. Tell her that he was in charge now, and she didn't have to deal with any of this.

She called the surgeon's office the moment they got home to see if it was even possible to have the surgery date moved up.

Dr. Catterson's nurse was, as she'd been from the very first appointment, kind and understanding but professional, which Jessie appreciated. "I do think it will relieve some of your stress to have it behind you," she said. "Let me check the schedule, and I'll call you back."

"Okay," Jessie said, but the nurse had already disconnected. All business, but that was the only way to be. Now that she had made the call, Jessie felt more in control than she had for the past week. All she had to do now was wait.

She still hadn't told the kids, or her mom, or her siblings. Or friends. No one, actually, other than Greg. *How do you tell people you love that you have cancer?* she wondered. It wasn't just changing her life; it was going to change theirs. It would move to the top of whatever worries they were already dealing with in day-to-day life.

Their youngest child, Hunter, would be the hardest to tell. True, he was in his twenties and on his own, but he was still—and always would be—their baby. He would be home from college for the weekend, and she and Greg had already decided to talk to him then, in person. That way, he could see that she was okay, and they could see that he was okay.

Then, they would tell Matthew and Libby, so they could be there for their little brother. Jessie knew Hunter would more openly express his feelings with his siblings than with his parents, regardless of how close they were. That was okay. It was a good thing.

She looked down at the calendar on her lap, the dates blurry. She didn't notice the tears on her cheeks until the ringing phone jolted her out of her thoughts. Dr. Catterson's nurse began talking the second Jessie picked up the receiver.

"This never happens," she said, "but one of our patients has to postpone her surgery. She has the flu. We can do your surgery on Wednesday. You'll need to be there really early for blood work, and surgery will be at nine that morning. Hospital admissions will call you with more information, as they won't have time to mail you the paperwork." The nurse sounded a little breathless, happy even, to deliver the news that the surgery could be moved up by months.

Jessie sank back into the chair. The surgery would be in a few days? Oh, God. This was real. "Can I have a day or two to talk to Greg?"

The line was silent for a split second before the nurse answered. "Well, no. Actually, you can't. If you don't want this time slot, there are other women who do."

Jessie could hear frustration in the nurse's voice. She had practically begged to have the surgery date moved up, and now she was hesitating. Why?

"Okay." Her voice was barely more than a whisper. Jessie hated that she suddenly felt so indecisive, so unsure. That wasn't like her. The momentary feeling of being in control was gone.

"All right, then," the nurse answered. "The hospital will call with details and the time they need you there. You said you wanted to have the implants at the same time, so I'll call the plastic surgeon and get you an appointment with her on Monday or Tuesday. I'll try to get you an appointment on the same day with the oncologist so you can discuss chemotherapy. I'll call back as soon as I have that set up."

Jessie was numb. *Oh, God*, she thought again. *Oh, God.* This was happening quicker than time allowed her to get mentally prepared. Somewhere in the back of her mind, she had held on to a sliver of hope that this might be—could still turn out to be—a mistake. Maybe Dr. Ames was wrong. Maybe Dr. Catterson was wrong. Maybe all of the tests were wrong.

But she knew they weren't. What hadn't seemed real from the first moment she'd answered the phone less than a week ago had now become the only constant in her life—always there, lurking in the background, and waiting to jump out as she visited with acquaintances at the post office, the grocery store, on the street. It threatened to take over when she talked with friends on the phone or when she put on makeup and saw the new tension on her face in the mirror.

Sometimes she wondered if others could sense a difference in her. Did she look different? Act different? Could they guess that she had something unimaginable growing inside her body?

It felt like she was carrying around a horrible secret. Well, she was, and she didn't want to let it out, didn't want anyone to look at her with sorrow in their eyes.

She sat down at the kitchen table, still holding the now-quiet phone. She had just agreed to have major surgery in a matter of days. The decision alone seemed to have drained all of the energy from her body. She needed to call Greg. She hated the words she would have to say, but he would have to arrange to take a few days off. She had wanted to get this over as quickly as possible. She'd gotten her wish.

Thinking of the days ahead, Jessie realized she didn't fear the surgery as much as she dreaded the first meeting with a plastic surgeon and an oncologist. Just thinking of their titles was daunting. She'd previously seen her family doctor once a year for a physical; now Jessie had more medical appointments than she could even conceive.

Greg, again, was terrific. "Good deal" was his response when Jessie called to tell him the new schedule.

She tried explaining her fears to Greg when he got home that night. "I don't know if I've even truly accepted the reality that I have breast cancer," she said. "Everything is just going too fast."

"Let's get going on this, and get it behind you," he replied, pulling her close. "Everything is going to be okay, Jess. I know it is."

The tightening of his jaw and the brightness in his eyes had Jessie wondering if he really believed that was true.

Chapter 7

Irene looked up from the magazine on her lap each time a new woman entered the waiting room. During her months of coming to Dr. Catterson, she had decided to make it her purpose to put the women at ease, as much as was possible anyway, considering the location. No one came to a breast cancer clinic for fun.

As one young woman took a seat, Irene offered her a sincere smile. The patient was so young. "I like your boots," Irene said, knowing from past experience that steering the conversation away from why each of them was here helped ease the tension. "They look warm and comfortable."

The woman smiled, her face suddenly brightening and the fear lessening. "Thank you. They are both of those things, actually." Then she added, almost apologetically, "I kind of splurged on them."

Irene liked this unpretentious, pretty young woman. "You're allowed," she said but then wished she hadn't. The mood that had been verging on lightheartedness a second ago returned to reality.

Marcie's smile dimmed. "Yeah, I guess so," she said.

Before Irene could think of something to say to get the lighter mood back, another woman, who had been checking in at the nurse's station, took a seat. She seemed familiar, and Irene wondered if she'd seen her here before. Probably. The woman looked tired, with dark circles under her eyes.

"I heard you talking about your boots," Jessie said, smiling at the young woman beside her. "I like them, too. They'll last forever. I have a similar pair but didn't wear them today. I couldn't decide if it was cold enough. I know most women don't wear socks with them, but I like to, and my feet sizzle unless it's twenty degrees below zero."

All of the women laughed, and Irene said, "I'd love to have a pair of boots, but I've always thought maybe they were too young-looking for me."

"Nothing is too young-looking," Jessie said. "Anything goes these days. You should get some. You'd love them."

Irene was enjoying the interaction. Sometimes the other women who were waiting to see Dr. Catterson made it quite clear by their body language that they didn't want conversation. They had enough to deal with. She understood and respected that. Once in a while, a woman would ask questions, as if Irene was the go-to source for answers. She knew she was older than most of the other women she'd seen here, but she resented the attitude that they could ask her anything. Like where she was in treatment, what it had been like, and what her prognosis was. She always steered those conversations to something else, hoping the woman asking such personal and pointed questions would get the hint. She was evidently pretty good at doing that, since those conversations usually ground to a halt.

She made a personal note in her head to stick to comments about clothing in the future. She was enjoying these two women and wondered if she'd see them again. Dr. Catterson's patients often had their surgeries at different hospitals and started their treatments at different centers. Although they all eventually came back here for checkups, different schedules meant it was unlikely they would see the same people again. Still, it was possible.

The conversation about fuzzy winter boots led the women into talking about how great it would be in a few months when the weather warmed up, and they'd be wearing shorts and sandals again.

"It'll be nice to get the kids out of coats, hats, gloves, and boots," Marcie said. "I'm pretty tired of cleaning up puddles of melted snow."

Her words could have been taken as a complaint, but it was obvious she enjoyed being a mom.

"What children do you have?" Irene asked. It was a topic she usually avoided, but it seemed to fit today.

"Three," Marcie answered. "Two girls and a boy. All under the age of eight."

Jessie smiled at the young woman. "We have three as well, but for us, it's two boys and a girl. And they're all in their twenties now, but I remember those days of winter clothes stacked up in the hallway. Enjoy them; the time goes so fast. I can hardly believe our children are all adults now."

Marcie turned to Irene. "What about you? Do you have children?"

The question typically made Irene wince. Even with women's liberation (did people still use that term?), a woman without children was something of an oddity, especially for her generation.

"I don't," she answered. "One of my biggest regrets. Of course, women of my age thought they had to be married first, so two big regrets, I guess. Although, I admire women who become mothers on their own—no man needed."

Irene quickly added with a bright smile, "Well, you know what I mean."

Marcie and Jessie both laughed.

The women were still sharing the lighthearted camaraderie when a nurse appeared holding a chart and called Jessie's name. The mood immediately became sober, as if the women suddenly remembered where they were—and why. Jessie smiled slightly at the other two women and followed the nurse out of the waiting room. She was there for blood work before surgery the following morning, surgery to have a mastectomy.

A different nurse called Marcie's name within a few seconds, and Marcie too offered Irene a hint of a smile. "I enjoyed visiting with you," she said and, in a quieter voice, added, "Thank you." She would learn the results of the MRI today, her place on a test that could immediately—and forever—change her life.

Irene watched the two women leave, feeling a quick flash of sorrow, and wished she'd been courageous enough to give each of them a quick hug, but the time had passed. Both women had disappeared from her sight.

She sat for a moment, closing the magazine and replacing it on the small side table beside her chair, and realized the women hadn't exchanged names. *Well*, she mused, *that was probably the least important part to our meeting.*

Another woman entered the center and stood at the nurses' station, waiting for someone to help her. Irene thought for a second about staying, but the morning had fatigued her; plus, she wanted to hold close the memory of the other two women, their conversations, and their laughter.

She stooped to pick up her carry-all from the floor beside the chair and walked toward the door. She didn't have any appointments today. There was no reason for her to linger in Dr. Catterson's waiting room. The staff had become accustomed to her unscheduled visits and smiled as she waved a quick good-bye.

Irene sent a silent prayer toward the exam rooms, where she knew other women sat. She hoped she'd been able to help two of them this morning.

Chapter 8

Jessie and Greg were enjoying having their son Hunter home from college for the weekend, but by Saturday evening, they still hadn't said anything to him about the upcoming surgery. It was actually painful for Jessie to watch him joke and laugh, not knowing his mom was keeping a dreaded secret. Although their younger son was nearly a grown man now, she could still see the little boy in him. He had always been impish, relishing life with gusto and making the most common activity an event, a memory to cherish.

Watching Hunter joke with a friend from elementary school who had stopped by, Jessie was surprised to remember what the family had come to call "the Ninja Turtle event." The five of them had gone to an amusement park, but Hunter had been too little to go on any of the rides, other than those he had deemed were "for babies." But he loved the games of chance. Jessie and Greg kept giving him dollars to try for a giant stuffed Ninja Turtle. Even at the age of six, Hunter had excelled at sports. He was consistently the highest scorer on the town's Pee Wee League soccer team. He held his own playing with much older boys on the basketball court in the park and loved to run everywhere. But try as he might, he couldn't knock over the weighted milk bottles to win the stuffed animal. Greg had tried explaining to him that the game was likely rigged so that it was nearly impossible for anyone to win. Greg, Matthew, and even Libby had tried to win the stuffed toy with no luck. Hunter had fallen asleep in the backseat on the way home, exhausted from a day of fun—and from crying at his failure to win the coveted prize.

Then Greg had suddenly turned into the parking lot of a discount store. He dashed inside, telling Jessie and the older kids that he wanted to check on something and would be back in a second. True to his word, he was gone for only a short time and came back with his arms full of a giant stuffed Ninja Turtle. They hadn't been able to "win" it, but Greg had been determined that his little boy would have it. They had propped it up beside Hunter so that he'd see it the second he opened his eyes. And he had, exclaiming in boyish excitement that he loved it more than anything in the whole wide world. They still had it, stuffed into a black plastic trash bag in the attic, along with other remnants of his childhood. Jessie always thought that maybe he'd want to share the story with his own son someday.

She tried to fight the idea that crept into her mind: *I might not be here when Hunter becomes a father.* She loved their children equally, but as her last baby, Hunter would always hold a special place in her heart and in her life. She loved having him back home, even if it was only for a short visit. Jessie hated that this trip home would be marked by what she was about to tell him. She wished she could solve this problem as easily as buying him a stuffed turtle.

"I'm going out with the guys," Hunter announced on Saturday night. "I won't be late, but don't wait up. It'll probably be after ten-thirty." He laughed at the joke between them. Jessie and Greg rarely stayed up past the ten o'clock news.

They had just finished eating enchiladas, one of Hunter's favorite foods. Jessie was sitting on the arm of a big overstuffed chair, waiting to clean up the kitchen after the guys moved to the family room. She looked up pleadingly to Greg, where he stood behind their son at the kitchen counter. She couldn't delay this any longer. Hunter was going out for the evening and would head back to school in the morning.

How could she do this? How did people do this?

"We need to talk to you for a second before you go," Jessie said, looking to Greg for support. He nodded encouragement, his eyes steady on hers.

Hunter leaned back against the counter. "What's up?" The familiar lightheartedness in his eyes dimmed, as if he knew something bad was about to happen. Jessie hated to be the cause of that.

She remembered telling Hunter when each of his grandfathers had died. That had been hard, really hard, but he had expected the news those times. They all had. This was harder.

She tried to keep her voice as matter-of-fact as she could.

Hunter's eyes never left hers as she explained that a routine mammogram—a test that she had every year, now that she was over forty—had showed something that shouldn't be there and that she was going to have surgery on Wednesday to have it taken care of. Everything was going to be okay. They just wanted him to know about it. Her son was a grown man, but still she avoided using the word "breast" and certainly didn't use the word "cancer."

Jessie knew she was talking too fast, trying to get all of the words out at once to put the moment behind them.

"It's not a big deal, really," she heard herself say. Why had she said that? It wasn't the truth, but she could hardly bear to see him so still, so intense.

His eyes were huge as he studied her face. His voice was unfamiliar, hard. "You have breast cancer?"

Jessie nodded, her eyes locked on her son's.

"That's a big deal, Mom. That's a real big deal." He sounded angry, and his posture stiffened, but Jessie knew him well enough to know it was a means to cope, until he could do so privately.

The room was silent.

Jessie stood up and gave Hunter a quick hug. She avoided looking at Greg. She had handled this horribly. And it couldn't be undone. If she saw tenderness in Greg's eyes now, she knew she'd fall apart. She couldn't do that. Not yet.

She took a step back so that she could look up at Hunter. "No, you're right. It *is* a big deal. I don't know why I even said that it wasn't. It is something serious, but I'm going to be fine. We found it early; the doctors will take care of it; and I'm going to be okay. I am."

Then came his questions. How long had she known? Why hadn't they told him sooner? Did his brother and sister know? Who else knew?

Greg answered for her. "We knew you'd be home this weekend, and we would be able to tell you in person. You're the only one we've talked to so far, but we'll call your brother and sister, now that you know."

"Tonight?"

Jessie knew he needed to talk to them, to process this change in life.

"Yes," Greg answered. "We'll call them tonight."

***Telling difficult** news to someone face-to-face is overrated,* Jessie thought. Telling Hunter had been terrible. Telling the other kids, her mom, her brother, and her sister over the phone had been a little easier. On her end, anyway. She wondered what they had each done after they had hung up. The kids probably called each other to see if they had each gotten exactly the same news or if any one of them had any more insight than the others. They likely discussed what they should do now. Should they be there for the surgery? If asked, Jessie was prepared to tell them no; it was best if they weren't there. There wasn't any point, actually, and she didn't want to be worrying about them while she was going into major surgery.

She had soft-coated the news to her mom, never saying the C-word.

"Good morning. What are you up to today?" she asked when her mom answered the phone.

"You just caught me," her mom said. "I'm running to the store to get ingredients to make a cake. I don't know if you remember John Williams. He was at the bank when you were still home. Anyway, his brother passed away."

Jessie tried to listen, but her mind raged ahead to what she would have to say. She cut her mom off before the conversation could turn to Mr. Williams's surviving family members and funeral arrangements.

"I hate to have this conversation over the phone, Mom, but I wanted to let you know. A mammogram showed a lump in my right breast, and then they found another one in the left breast."

The silence at the other end of the phone line had Jessie rushing to finish the call. "I'll be fine. They're going to take them out in the morning. I'm sorry I didn't tell you sooner, but there has been so much to take care of, and we just got the surgery scheduled."

"Oh, Jess." Her mom's voice was quiet, frightened.

She could hear in her mother's tone that she knew it was more serious than Jessie was telling. But her mom accepted the words as offered, saying she knew Jessie was strong.

"You'll be fine, honey," her mother said. "I'm glad you have Greg to help you through this. I wish I could be there with you, too."

"I know, Mom. But it will all be okay." Her mom lived three hundred miles away, and although she still drove, Jessie wouldn't encourage her to make that long of a trip. "I'll call you after the surgery, as soon as I can."

Jessie hung up the phone and walked outside. *I didn't handle that very well either*, she thought. What was wrong with her? Other than the obvious. She had ended the call quickly, not wanting to answer questions or give her mom time to begin crying. She didn't have the energy to comfort someone else. Maybe there was a book or a website that explained how to tell loved ones that you have what could be a terminal disease. And that you don't know what is going to happen and that you are scared out of your mind. *Well*, she thought, *it's too late to search for that help now*.

Her siblings had taken the news as expected. She and her sister, Bethany, were so different from their brother, Will, that through the years they'd often joked that maybe they weren't really biologically related at all.

Jessie called Will first, knowing that would be an easier phone call than the one to her sister. She gave him an abbreviated version of what had been going on; she was just calling to let him know she was having surgery.

"The mom of a friend of mine found a lump in her breast and had a biopsy, and it had turned out to be nothing," Will answered in his take-charge way. "Yours is probably nothing, too."

"Well, no. It is something, Will," Jessie quietly answered. She had no desire or emotional strength to get into a breast-lump competition. No winner there. She understood her brother was only trying to let her know it would be okay, but really, did they know that?

Bethany, closer to Jessie in age and in temperament, had, as expected, been devastated. "Oh, Jessie. Oh, no. What can I do? I'll come up and be with Greg during surgery. It's going to be all right. I know it will."

The positive tone in Beth's words was soothing, despite the underlying fear in her voice.

"It will," Jessie agreed. "I just wish it was over, you know? I don't know for sure what comes next, though. Chemo, I guess."

"How long have you known about this?" Beth asked the question that was apparently foremost in everyone's mind.

"Only a week."

"A week? You've known you have breast cancer for a week, and you're just now telling me? Jess, come on."

Jessie could hear the anger in Beth's voice and smiled. Anger was good.

"I know. I'm sorry," Jessie said. "It's all been a blur. We wanted to tell the kids first. And I thought I'd have time to talk to you in person. The surgery wasn't going to be for a couple of months, but I decided to move it up, and now it's Wednesday."

"Wednesday? This Wednesday? Oh, Jess."

"I really just want Greg with me," Jessie said quickly, before Bethany could argue. She could mentally picture her sister looking at a calendar, figuring out what activities she would need to rearrange or cancel. Her only daughter was getting married in a few weeks. Jessie knew Beth had enough on her plate as it was.

Surprisingly, Beth said she understood, and Jessie smiled at her sister's closing comment: "Feel me hugging you." It was something they had repeated to each other throughout their lives. And she did feel the hug through the phone line.

Jessie assured her sister, as much as she could, that it would be best if Beth went on about her daily life; they would keep her in the know.

And Jessie knew, without her sister's saying another word, that they both wondered what the future would hold—and if there would be a future for them to share.

Chapter 9

Monday morning started with the appointment with the plastic surgeon to pick out breast implants. *And the weirdness continues*, Jessie thought. The doctor smiled when she told Jessie, "Some women use this opportunity to go larger." Jessie answered that she would be perfectly happy if they could just come close to replicating her real breasts. Plus, going larger than a size B would require more surgery. More pain. More recovery time. A size B would be just fine.

She and Greg then drove to the appointment with an oncologist who had been recommended to them. First, however, they were to talk with a "breast navigator."

"Now there's a job title," Greg joked as they sat in the hospital waiting room. It amazed Jessie that in the course of only a week, since the diagnosis, they were able to find tidbits of humor in all of this.

The receptionist explained that the navigator worked with women diagnosed with breast cancer, helping to steer them through the obstacle course of specialists, options in treatment, and decision making.

"Still," Greg said, making both Jessie and the receptionist laugh, "is that the best title they could come up with?"

It didn't help that this particular "navigator" was a skinny, birdlike woman with brittle bleached hair and too much makeup, who flitted into the tiny exam room and spent the first fifteen minutes of their appointment talking about herself. She shared how she had gotten into this field and how blessed she was to be able to help women. She just loved her job. Felt it was a calling.

Jessie assumed the woman's training had included a class on trying to put patients facing major surgery at ease, because she had been "called" to help them. If so, it wasn't working. Either that, or this was bird-woman's first day on the job, and she was doing a terrible job of it.

Jessie didn't care how much this creepy woman enjoyed her work. She wasn't there to make the woman feel good.

"On a scale of one to ten, with ten being the highest, how would you rate your level of stress?" Bird-woman picked up her pen to check the appropriate box on a yellow form attached to her clipboard, and smiled gaily at Jessie.

Seriously? Jessie thought. The anger that had become familiar to her over the past week simmered.

"Ten," she replied.

Jessie's answer actually seemed to excite the navigator. The woman leaned forward and placed a scrawny hand on Jessie's knee. "Why do you think your stress level is a ten? Where do you think this stress is coming from?"

Jessie could feel the heat in her face. She knew she was suddenly angrier than she had been throughout this entire ordeal, and that was saying something. Although she'd been raised her entire life to be nice to others, Jessie thought, *The hell with that.*

Jessie could feel Greg's anxiety without looking at him. She turned and faced the navigator, carefully enunciating her answer. "Because I have breast cancer. Because I'm facing major surgery to have my breasts removed. Because I'm facing chemotherapy, and that's really frightening. I know it will make feel crappy and that I'll probably lose all of my hair. And because after all of that, I still won't know how this is going to end. I don't know what all of this is going to do to my life or to the lives of the people I love. And because I don't want to die."

Bird-woman's training evidently hadn't included how to respond to those statements. Her reaction to Jessie's outburst was to pretend it had never happened. "Is it the financial aspect that is causing you stress?" she asked, leaning back in her chair, clearly putting some distance between her and the patient.

"The financial aspect?" Jessie repeated, now stealing a glance at Greg, who looked as if he'd rather be strung out naked on an ant hill than be in this exam room. She could see the fear in his eyes as to how she might react to this awful woman. He knew his wife well. "I really don't give a shit about the financial aspect," Jessie answered. "That is absolutely the least of my worries. I hadn't even thought about it until now, not for one second, until you brought it up."

The navigator evidently decided she had enough information. She stood, told them the doctor would be with them in a few minutes, and left the room.

"Good grief," Greg muttered.

The next visit—this one with the oncologist—wasn't much better. He had evidently talked with the navigator.

"I understand that you are feeling some stress," he said, smiling at Jessie. "Perhaps I can alleviate some of that by answering your questions." He then proceeded to take numerous phone calls and answer several text messages while Jessie was formulating questions in her mind. Just as she would begin to ask one, his beeper would sound again.

Sensing the growing tension in the room, the doctor finally smiled at Jessie and magnanimously announced he would just let his service know he was with a patient.

"Good call," Jessie said, surprising the doctor and Greg—and herself as well. She stood and told the oncologist, as politely as possible at the moment, that it had been a long day. To Greg, she said, "There have to be other oncologists."

Without saying another word, Jessie and Greg walked out of the room.

Jessie knew her actions bordered on rudeness, but what a good decision. She felt stronger, physically and emotionally. The outburst had been coming, she realized, and it felt good. She would consider her never having to see the navigator again as one of the blessings in this process. Perhaps the woman was a help to others, but Jessie preferred to navigate this rough terrain without that kind of assistance. Greg agreed, but Jessie wondered later if it was out of mutual feelings toward the person or out of fear of his wife.

Dr. Catterson recommended a different oncologist, one that both Greg and Jessie liked immediately. Jessie thought that liking her cancer-treatment doctor probably wasn't essential, but it would certainly help. Dr. Park gave them his undivided attention, explained the process in understandable language, and answered all of their questions without showing an ounce of pity. That was essential too, in Jessie's mind. He was matter-of-fact, even booting up his laptop to show Jessie and Greg the survival rates for breast cancer patients and how those rates had improved drastically over the past decade.

His use of the phrase "survival rate" shocked them into reality. Dr. Park took Jessie's hand and squeezed it hard.

"This isn't going to be easy, Jessie," he said. "I won't lie to you. But you're a strong woman. You'll get through this and go on with life. You're going to be fine."

"I hope so," Jessie answered. Her eyes searched his for any sign that he was giving them pat responses.

"You are going to be fine," he said again, and he sounded so sure, so firm in his answer that Jessie felt he might be right.

They followed Dr. Park down the hallway to the treatment center, where he introduced them to the staff. Susan, the center's director, and the nurses in their colorful scrubs seemed the right mix of professionalism and compassion.

"Let me show you around," Susan said and then laughed. "Well, you can see most of it from here." She waved her arms to indicate the open room.

Jessie only glanced at the space, her eyes both wild and resigned. She didn't want to be here, but she knew she'd soon spend countless and unforgettable hours in this room. Like it or not.

Susan seemed unfazed by Jessie's frozen stance. Taking her arm, she led her to the group of black recliners that lined the room's perimeter and introduced her to the women sitting there. Each was anchored to the spot by intravenous lines that snaked from metal poles stationed beside the chairs to some spot beneath their blouses and sweatshirts.

To Jessie, it looked like something from a B-rated horror movie, but Susan seemed at ease. She first introduced Greg and Jessie to a woman named Irene, who seemed to be older than the rest of the women, although it was hard to tell. Something about the woman seemed familiar, but Jessie couldn't imagine how they would know each other. Besides, she couldn't see very much of her. A knitted cap covered Irene's head. Her nose and mouth were hidden behind a white mask. Irene nodded, and Jessie wondered if the woman was smiling. The crinkles at the sides of her eyes above the mask hinted that maybe she was. Irene was covered with a thin white blanket, and Jessie had the impression that she was a tiny woman, but, again, it was hard to tell much about her. Jessie smiled, hoping the woman was smiling back. She had a momentary feeling of sympathy for Irene and then coldly realized she herself was no different from this stranger. In a matter of days, she'd be sitting beside her.

Jessie followed Susan's turn toward another woman, whom she introduced as Karen. The woman's posture indicated she was indignant at being introduced second.

"Well, welcome to the world of breast cancer," she said, a sharp edge to her voice.

The words themselves and the anger evident in them took Jessie by surprise. She was thinking of some way to answer the woman when Susan saved her the effort by turning to walk back toward the office, motioning for Jessie to follow.

Looking back to the treatment room, Jessie wondered which recliner would be hers when she came back in a few days to start her own chemo treatments.

She didn't intend to make friends here, but the hours would at least be bearable if she could sit by someone whose company she enjoyed. She doubted that would be Karen.

With the plastic surgeon and oncologist appointments over and a tour of the chemo room behind them, there was nothing to do now but wait. Jessie and Greg drove home in silence, both lost in their own thoughts and unable to share them. Greg reached over several times to squeeze his wife's hand and then turned back to driving.

The whole thing still seemed like a bad dream to Jessie, as if she were researching breast cancer to write a newspaper article. Over the years, she had interviewed countless strangers following tragedies: home fires, car wrecks, and natural disasters. If she was honest with herself, she'd never really given much thought to what those people were going through. She just collected the information and looked forward to being back at her desk, where she could add adjectives and adverbs and write a touching story. She'd kept herself emotionally detached, she realized, and now, she was working to distance herself from all of this as well.

The evening was as quiet as the ride home had been. The television was on, but neither of them would later be able to say what shows they had watched.

Before changing into her pajamas, Jessie thought that perhaps a bath would calm her frayed nerves and help her to sleep. She filled the tub with lavender bubble bath from a huge plastic bottle, a gift from one of the kids, years ago, that she hadn't had the heart to discard. She sank into the warm and fragrant water, leaned back on the porcelain, and let the tears fall.

She thought of the women she had met in the treatment room. Karen and Irene, if she remembered correctly. She prided herself at being good at remembering names, an occupational side effect for journalists. Karen had seemed downright rude. Irene, who seemed familiar, even under the gauze mask, looked as if she just wanted to be left alone. Jessie could understand that. She hoped none of the women would want to visit during her treatments. She hated small talk. She wondered if the room had Wi-Fi. If it did, she'd be able to play games on her e-reader or watch a movie.

Feeling somewhat calmer or at least resigned to what was to come, she climbed from the tub and toweled off. She reached for the bottle of lotion and began smoothing it over her arms and shoulders, stopping suddenly when she came to her breasts. Looking up at her reflection in the mirror, the tears started again. It occurred to her that this would be the last day of having her own breasts. It was such a strange thought. She was immediately overwhelmed with sorrow that the body she had been born with, the body she had watched mature and change through childhood, adolescence, and into adulthood, would soon be altered in a manner she couldn't fathom.

Chapter 10

The feeling of sorrow returned as she stood in front of the mir- ror in the tiny hospital bathroom the following day. The mastectomy had been performed at nine in the morning, as scheduled, and Jessie had slept off the anesthesia until almost noon. The nurses told her that Greg had sat beside her for all of those hours, and when she was finally able to stay awake for more than a few minutes, Jessie urged him to get out of the hospital.

"Why don't you go get something to eat?" she suggested. "You have to be starved." They had shared an early light supper the night before and had gotten up when the alarm clock on Greg's cell phone beeped at 4:15 a.m. Jessie had checked into the hospital at six o'clock. All of that seemed weeks ago.

"Are you sure? I could just grab something from the cafeteria," Greg said.

"Go, please. I'm fine," Jessie insisted.

After he left, she managed to sit up for a few minutes and then, holding on to the side bars of the hospital bed, forced herself to stand. She made her way into the tiny bathroom. No doubt she was supposed to wait for a nurse, but she wanted to see the results of the surgery for herself. By herself.

I look horrible, she thought, standing in front of the mirror over the sink. The fluorescent lighting turned her skin a sick shade of yellow. Her cheeks were flushed and blotchy, her eyes looked sunken, and her hair was tired and limp. Ignoring her face, she carefully lifted the hospital gown, surprised to find there were no bandages covering her breasts—or what was left of them. She stared at the thin lines across both and wondered if the surgeon had used sutures or glue. Dried dark blood bordered the lines. She looked flat, although she was supposed to be the same size as she'd been prior to surgery, thanks to the implants. Had they forgotten to put them in? Small tubes led out from the sides of both breasts to small plastic containers where rusty liquid pooled.

Dr. Catterson had told her what to expect, but seeing it was shattering. Her body looked mutilated. She was too shocked to cry. She quickly pulled the gown down and made her way back to the bed, just as a nurse walked in.

"Well, look who's up!" the nurse said with a bright smile. "You should have buzzed if you wanted to get out of bed, but it looks like you did all right by yourself. How are you feeling?"

"I don't know." Jessie tried to smile but failed. "Tired, I guess. A little depressed." She fought back tears and climbed gingerly back into the bed.

The nurse helped her in and touched her arm. "That's very normal. You've been through a lot. The doctor will be in to see you soon. Your surgery went well, and now that's all behind you."

Jessie tried to feel good about that. The ugly alien was removed from her body. But it had taken so much with it. She had known what bilinear mastectomy meant. She'd heard it from Dr. Catterson. She'd looked it up online and had seen the ugly photos. What had she expected?

Turning her face away from the nurse, Jessie let her tears fall unchecked until her hospital gown and sheets were wet. She hadn't allowed herself to think about what happened during the surgery; she'd been focused only on getting the cancer out of her.

Well, it was gone. Along with her breasts. Along with her womanhood. Forget sexuality. There was nothing sexy about what she had just seen in the bathroom mirror.

The nurse silently helped her into a fresh hospital gown, put clean sheets on the bed, took her vital signs, and left the room. Jessie was glad the nurse hadn't offered platitudes, but maybe that would have helped. It had only been a few hours since the surgery. Everything—her body and life in general—would look better in a few days. She hoped.

Jessie slid back out of the bed as soon as the door quietly closed on its own and reached for her makeup from inside her overnight bag. By the time Greg returned, she had combed her hair and had applied foundation, blush, and mascara.

"Wow, you look better," he said, leaning over the hospital bed to give her a quick kiss. "How are you feeling?"

"Good, actually," Jessie lied. "I've been out of bed a couple of times."

Greg looked at her tenderly. "Really? Already? That's great. You look so much better. Sore?"

Jessie knew he was asking about her breasts, and she thought about seeing her changed body in the mirror. "Not really," she answered. "Just tired." She turned her head away, feigning sleep.

Dr. Catterson checked on her at about four o'clock that afternoon and said if Jessie was feeling up to it, she could go home. Everything had gone well, as expected, she said, and Jessie only needed to rest and regain her strength. She wanted to see Jessie the following week.

Greg drove carefully, braking gently at stoplights and accelerating more slowly than he normally would. Jessie appreciated the gesture, but she wished he'd drive faster. She wanted to get home. They had given her strong pain medication prior to her dismissal from the hospital, and she could feel the pills kicking in. She wanted to be in her pajamas, in her own bed, before she completely conked out.

They'd been gone from home for less than a day, but everything was different.

When they'd moved up the surgery date, Greg had promised her that she would be okay for her niece's wedding. She wasn't. Weddings were events for hugging. Hugging the happy couple. Hugging the parents. The groomsmen. The bridesmaids. The flower girls. Friends. Strangers. Jessie cringed any time someone came near her. Shaking hands seemed a little cold on such a happy occasion, so she opted for being the first one to lean in for a cheek press, hoping a hug wouldn't need to follow that absurd move. Mostly, it didn't. But it didn't stop her from wondering if everyone was checking out her chest to see what was there. Or what wasn't. She wondered who among the crowd of people knew she had had a mastectomy. Her mother had probably told friends and had likely had Jessie's name added to the church prayer list. Beth surely had told her close friends. Will? Probably not. She didn't know about the kids. Matthew, Libby, and Hunter seemed to be having the time of their life, dancing, drinking, and acting silly together. Jessie loved watching them, but too frequently, one or all three came to the table to check on her.

Jessie repeatedly tried—and failed every time—to tell herself the wedding wasn't about her, for heaven's sake. It was about the happy couple, about Beth and this important time in her life. But since that phone call in the kitchen, it seemed as if everything was about Jessie. How was she, really? Was she getting enough rest? What came next? No one visited with her about the weather.

She looked forward to the day when she wouldn't be defined by cancer.

The mastectomy had been only a couple of weeks earlier. She hadn't started chemo yet and, surprisingly, she felt pretty good. She was still a little sore in her armpits, and the scars across both breasts were red and raised, but she rubbed cream onto them every night. Her favorite sleeping shirt had two obvious dark spots on them where the cream hit, reminding her of the stains from leaked milk when she had been breastfeeding, which again had her crying in the shower every morning.

Jessie barely recognized her own body. Her new breasts were certainly not the ones where her babies had cuddled or that her husband had made love to. Still, having opted for implant surgery at the same time as the mastectomy meant she wasn't completely flat. She tried to think positively: Her new breasts were nice and firm. There was that. At least now—and for the first time since she'd been a teenager—she could confidently go braless under a T-shirt and no longer have to worry about straps showing with sleeveless tops or dresses.

She was eager to go shopping for a new bra for her smaller size. The smallest bras always seemed the prettiest in stores anyway, designed in exciting, fun colors and styles.

"Let's wait on that," Dr. Catterson had suggested in a kind tone when Jessie had mentioned her plans. "Your breasts are still changing, and I don't want you wearing anything constrictive. No wires, for sure. Let's stay with the sports bras for a while, okay?"

At night, after Greg was asleep, Jessie would slip from bed to stand in the clear night air on the deck. Looking up to her three bright stars, she'd repeat the mantra she had designed for herself: I'm healthy. I'm healing. I'm happy. And I am strong.

A few weeks down the road, she added a roar at the end, reminding her of the feeble childlike roar from baby Simba in *The Lion King*, one of her favorite movies. When Katy Perry came out with her song "Roar," Jessie had smiled to herself every time she heard it. It became her personal fight song. The words and the music made her feel stronger.

She was finding that the simplest things made her smile: Toenails painted bright green. A colorful, fat ceramic robin by the front door. Funny greeting cards, both those she sent and those she received.

A card she had received from Bethany showed two old ladies, one of them buttoning up an out-of-style cardigan. The wording inside read, "Mabel, don't you think it's a little early in the day to wear your 'do me' sweater?" It soon became a standing joke between the sisters. Jessie now had her favorite sweatshirt, dubbed as the 'do me' sweatshirt.

She wondered if her newfound appreciation for simple things was a reaction to thinking she might die. And if it was, so be it. It was an attitude she wanted to hold on to. She was thankful too for Greg's sense of humor, and it surprised her that they could laugh during any of this experience.

"No one asked me what size I wanted to order," he said with mock indignation, when Jessie admitted that maybe she was a little small on top.

"Yeah, well," Jessie had answered, "you get what you get, and you don't throw a fit." It was a line one of the kids had once repeated after a teacher had admonished her students for complaining. No fits allowed. It had become a familiar family joke through the years.

Jessie tried to hold on to that attitude. So she didn't have model breasts. Big deal. You get what you get.

The incisions across her breasts were healing, and there was little pain. She learned to dry quickly each morning after her shower and to put on a sports bra without looking at the mirror. With the bra on, she looked normal. Almost. Well, different, but okay.

Greg was still cautious around her new body, hugging her more gently, draping his arm across her shoulders in bed; in the past, he would have pulled her to him. He was as loving as always, just not physical, and while Jessie longed for that, she wondered how things would go with her new breasts. Time would tell, she guessed. They'd figure it out.

As the day to start chemo approached, the tension returned.

"I can go with you if you want me to," Greg said, but Jessie knew he'd rather not, and she couldn't blame him. She didn't know what it was going to be like, having poisonous chemicals pumped into her body. Would she feel sick immediately? Would it hurt? Plus, she didn't even know if husbands were allowed. She hadn't seen men there when they'd visited the treatment center before the surgery.

She gave Greg a tender smile and shook her head. "I know you would, but I think I'd rather just go alone."

"You can call me if you want me to come," he countered.

"Okay. Let's plan on that. If you don't hear from me, you'll know everything is fine." She caught her use of the word "fine" and offered Greg a wry grin. "Well, not fine. None of this is fine, but you know what I mean."

Chapter 11

Jessie didn't want to get out of her car. The rain didn't help. She watched watery ribbons flow down the windshield as she tried to recall what her dad had once told her about raindrops. Flat drops meant it would soon stop? Or was it thin streams? She couldn't remember. It wasn't raining hard, but it also didn't look as if it was going to stop any time soon. If she didn't get out now, she'd be late for her appointment. With a flip of her wrist, she turned off the radio, grabbed her keys from the ignition, and pushed open the car door. As she started toward the building, she looked back once to click the key fob, and then was reassured by the beep signaling that the vehicle was locked. She'd left her purse inside, which was something she never did, but this wasn't a shopping trip.

She carried the bright orange tote Bethany had given her, along with a matching crocheted throw. Her e-reader was tucked into one of the side pockets, along with mints, gum, and a bottle of water. Everything to make the next few hours easier, she hoped.

Jessie pushed open the heavy door marked with simple black-and-white lettering announcing it as the Cancer Treatment Center, and tried to ignore her reason for being here. She was functioning, barely, within the dark confines of a nightmare. When she did happen to see a glimpse of light and allowed herself to think that the worst might be over, the nightmare pulled her into ever darker and more frightening corridors that seemed to close behind her. She was in a battle with her own mind to not let fear of the unknown undermine the strength and courage she'd worked so hard to develop. *I'm healthy. I'm healing. And I'm strong*, she thought.

Looking straight ahead to the reception desk behind a sliding glass window, she walked to it and forced a smile. She was disappointed to not see Susan, the center's director and a familiar face. Instead, a young woman sat at the desk. She looked up as Jessie approached, sliding the window open to offer a smile.

Jessie tried to smile back. "Hi. I'm Jessie Gifford. I'm supposed to start . . . treatment . . . today." Her voice sounded weaker than she felt, and that surprised her. She physically couldn't say either of the "C–words"—chemo or cancer—and realized with a start that she didn't need to. Of course the staff knew precisely why she was there and what treatment she would have. She suddenly felt small, nearly invisible. She longed to go to the doctor and have the nurse ask, "So why are we seeing you today?" She didn't want to be here, to be a part of any of this.

Although she had toured the room only weeks ago, she hadn't really seen it. Her impression of it now resulted in a fresh wave of irritation, this time at the decorator. It was going to be hard enough to sit in one of the matching black vinyl recliners flanked by IV poles, staring at literature racks filled with titles of books on how to understand and accept chemotherapy and the changes to your body. But to be surrounded by walls painted a putrid shade of green? If what she'd always heard about the side effects of chemotherapy proved to be true, the sight of the walls wouldn't help either her mood or her stomach.

Thin white blankets were stacked in a large basket in front of a wooden screen. She wondered if the screen was there to block the view so those in the recliners wouldn't see normal life taking place down the hall, where nurses and office workers laughed at their stations. Maybe the screen was there to hide the patients in the chairs from people who were in the other part of the clinic, the part where babies were weighed, flu shots given, and sore throats checked. Whatever the reason, the screen didn't hide the fact that this wasn't a place to be by choice.

Jessie felt out of her comfort zone as she stood at the reception window, unsure of how to act. Maybe she should have visited here more often than her one quick stop and gotten more familiar with the surroundings, like a kindergarten roundup allowed five-year-olds to visit school before their parents left them there, but she doubted more visits would have done anything to put her at ease.

"We'll get you started in a second," the nurse said. "We're getting your IVs organized."

Jessie stared at the back of the screen where a pink poster promoting an upcoming Survivors' Walk had been taped. A survivor wasn't something she had ever aspired to be. She had *expected* to survive. Survive was what people did naturally. Until they were old, and then they didn't. Jessie had never thought of her life as something she had to work to survive. Until now, and it was a jolting thought. She had a disease that attached itself to the word survivor. Dr. Park's explanation of survival rates during her first meeting with him came to mind.

She hadn't wanted to hear the statistics then. She didn't want to hear them now either. Sure, she'd been sick in her life. And she knew people died of influenza or pneumonia or maybe even of serious colds, but she'd always been fortunate in regard to avoiding illnesses. She didn't even get an annual flu shot. She'd always taken her chances. She could count on one hand the number of times she had gotten ill enough to wonder if maybe she should miss work.

Well, here she was. One of the sick.

Waiting for the nurse, she studied the details on the poster as if they were the most intriguing words she'd ever read. Participants could walk for themselves or for someone they knew who had survived. Or hadn't. Jessie had always donated money to the walk at work. She knew coworkers who participated every year, creating a team and designing matching T-shirts. She remembered how they would excitedly plan to camp out together around the high-school track and discuss what snack foods each would bring. They looked forward to it, it seemed.

She always felt it was easier to give money, to feel like she had contributed and then to forget all about the whole thing. It was a foreign idea to realize *she* was now the subject of a nationwide awareness drive. People—strangers—were walking to support her.

Turning away from the poster, Jessie blinked back tears and forced what she hoped looked like a smile as a nurse in brightly colored scrubs approached. She carried a clipboard filled with papers that Jessie knew she was likely going to have to sign. *Let's get on with it*, she thought. *The sooner we get this started, the sooner it will be over and in the past.*

That's what the nurse had promised during the biopsy only weeks ago—that this would all be something she just had to go through for the next year or so, and then it would be in the past—only a memory—and she could get on with her life. She hoped the nurse was being truthful, and it wasn't just something she said to patients to give them hope and the courage to get through these months.

"I have a few papers for you to sign," the nurse said, "and I'll go through what drugs you'll be getting and what side effects to expect. Then we'll get you started. Today's infusion will be about three hours."

As she took a seat in one of the recliners, Jessie watched a woman walk down the long hallway, looking as if she was going to leave the center. Through her peripheral vision, Jessie realized the woman had taken a seat in the adjacent recliner instead and was listening and watching as the nurse went through the mountain of forms, having Jessie "sign here" and "here" and "here." The names of the drugs were impossible to decipher, and the nurse assured her that she would want to look over the papers more thoroughly after she got home, even giving her a clear plastic folder to "record the process."

I doubt it, Jessie thought. She was putting her life and her body in the hands of those who understood all of this.

That was their job, not hers. She already knew the plastic folder would be stuffed into a file drawer, or the bookcase, or maybe even into the trash the second she got home. She had no desire to read any of it.

If she'd learned anything in the past few weeks, it was that *not* knowing what to expect was the best way to go. For her, at least. Others might want to keep a personal diary of the experience and learn to say the names of the drugs going through their veins, killing both bad and good cells as they coursed along. They might participate in research studies, join a support group, and start a blog.

Jessie just wanted to get through it with some degree of sanity.

She tucked a strand of hair behind her ear and then partially unzipped the pink fleece top that would become her Thursday morning uniform for the foreseeable future. It was soft and warm and, more important, gave the nurse easy access to the catheter opening in her chest.

"Do you need to use the restroom before I start the IVs?" the nurse asked.

Jessie first answered no but then changed her mind. Three hours was a long time. The nurse directed her to the restroom down the hall, and after entering, Jessie turned from the door and stared at her reflection in the mirror over the sink. Her eyes looked huge. Her face was too pale. She barely recognized herself.

So it was starting. This was it.

She hoped that she wouldn't need to go to the bathroom again for the next three hours. What would that entail? Unhooking everything? Starting over? Calling for help?

Trying to not think about what was about to happen, Jessie returned to the green room and sat down in the recliner.

The nurse swabbed the thin skin covering the port with alcohol. "You'll feel a little prick," she warned, just as the needle was inserted. "Okay. I'll get this set, and you can just relax." The nurse plugged in the IV lines and handed Jessie the remote control for the TV. "Let us know if you need anything," she said and headed back behind the screen.

Jessie put her head back on the cool vinyl and closed her eyes. Her first round of chemo had started. Only three hours to go.

She was startled by someone touching her arm. Jessie looked to the next recliner, suddenly realizing she was fighting tears, and offered a slight smile to the woman she had watched walk down the hallway.

"I've been where you are," the woman said, giving Jessie a warm look. "It's a little overwhelming, isn't it? You just want to be somewhere else, huh?"

Jessie smiled back tentatively. "Anywhere else," she said.

Chapter 12

"Your first day, my last," the woman said to Jessie. "Look- ing back, it seems like it has gone quickly, but I know it doesn't feel that way to you right now. How many treatments? I heard the nurse call you Jessie. My name is Pam, by the way."

Jessie looked up at the stranger. Tears filled her eyes, and she had to clear her throat before she could answer. "Six, I think. Every Thursday for six weeks, if everything goes okay. Then, I'll get a different drug every three weeks for the rest of the year." Saying the schedule made it real, and she tried to smile but failed. "Sounds like forever."

Jessie realized she had listened to the nurse more closely than she had thought. And this woman had gone through all of this? Since Jessie had opted to keep the news of her breast cancer pretty much in the family, she hadn't had the opportunity to talk with anyone who had firsthand experience with all of this. Maybe that had been a mistake.

She realized she didn't want Pam to leave. There was something comfortable and unthreatening about her presence. Instinctively, Jessie knew it would be okay if she fell apart in front of this stranger. Finally, here was someone who would just talk in normal language about what she was going through. No confusing terms. No platitudes. Plus, Pam had survived all of this.

"So, you're done?" Jessie asked, swiping at her tears with the backs of her hands.

Pam gave her a tender smile and pulled the zipper up on what was obviously the top to a jogging suit, although she was wearing it with jeans. "Well, with chemo, anyway," she said. "I had a lumpectomy. Now I go for radiation. Every day for six weeks. Every day! The bad part is that you can't drive while you're having it, so I've had to call on my mom, my sister, and my friends to create a schedule to get me there and back. I hate that. Asking for help, I mean." Jessie was trying to think of what to say when Pam asked, "Did you get a wig yet? How do you like mine?"

The quick change in subjects made Jessie smile. "I do, actually. Have a wig, I mean. And I do like yours. I wasn't sure it was even a wig. It looks great."

Pam reached up nonchalantly and adjusted the sides of her wig. "Well, I had thought about going wild," she said. "You know, getting a long, black curly 'do or going red. But in the end, this one looks a lot like my real hair. Better, actually." She turned her head side to side, showing off the bouncy blonde curls swinging around her face.

"It's very natural-looking," Jessie said, wondering what else to tell someone about a wig. *For fake hair, it looks less fake than some?* Plus, she had no idea how the woman had looked before. But the wig did look good. In a different place, a different time, she probably wouldn't have given a thought to its being anything other than real hair.

Jessie was surprised how much more relaxed she suddenly felt. She leaned back into the recliner, less fearful now that she was talking with someone who had been through all of this and who looked good. Really good. And healthy. Normal. Happy.

She reached up and tucked strands of her own hair behind her ears. "I guess I'm hoping I'll be one of the lucky ones and not lose my hair, but my sister talked me into getting a wig, just in case," she said. "I feel like I'm playing dress-up, though, when I put it on. Plus, I still have my real hair. So I haven't worn it."

"Sixteen days," Pam said. Jessie looked at her quizzically, trying to figure out if they had jumped ahead again to some other conversation. Pam laughed at the bewildered look on Jessie's face. "That's how long it was for me after I started chemo until my hair fell out. Pretty much all at once. That was surprising. I guess I thought it would be a gradual thing. I know in movies it's pretty sudden, but I thought that was just in movies. You know, for timing. If I were you, I'd cut it as short as you can so it's not so much of a shock when it happens. Don't shave your head, though. Your scalp will hurt anyway from the drugs. Don't cause it any more trauma than necessary. Just clip it short."

Later, Jessie wondered what she had said to Pam after that. She hoped it had been nice and appropriate. She just didn't want to accept the loss of her hair as a sure thing. Pam seemed to think it was, and she was probably right. But Jessie held on to the thought that she would beat the odds, on that front anyway. She was due for some luck.

"I hope the morning goes fast for you," Pam said, pulling open the heavy door to the center. A blast of damp, chilly air rushed in. Then her new friend was gone.

Jessie realized too late that she should have wished the other woman well with radiation, but was that something one did? She wasn't sure if cancer had protocol.

She was sorry to see Pam leave. A different woman, the rude one—Jessie thought her name was Karen—had been in one of the other recliners while Jessie had filled out the paperwork and visited with Pam. She had evidently finished with her treatment for the day and waved a quick good-bye to Jessie as she left the center.

Another woman, this one young and cute with swingy dark hair, walked down the hall toward the treatment room. Jessie wasn't sure if she was one of the staff or a patient. *If she's a patient, she must not have started chemo yet*, Jessie thought. She knew the rooms farther down the hallway, beyond the screen, were for consultations. The woman gave Jessie a fragile smile as she walked past her, and then she too pushed open the heavy door and was gone.

Suddenly, Jessie remembered the woman. She was the one with the cute boots from Dr. Catterson's waiting room! She felt a jolt of excitement at seeing her again. They'd laughed that day, and Jessie had felt an immediately connection to her. And now they were both going through treatment at the same time. The thought sobered her instantly. They were both going through treatment—chemotherapy—because they both had breast cancer. She had fought off the sorrow and depression that threatened every moment of her days now, but the realization that this young, vibrant mother of three young children was going through this too was Jessie's undoing, and she choked back tears.

Jessie was thankful neither of the women said anything as they'd walked past. The fact that they hadn't offered words of reassurance gave Jessie an unexpected kindred feeling toward them. They got it.

Jessie eyed the blankets stacked in a basket in the corner. The room was chilly, but she didn't want to buzz for a nurse. She settled for pulling the fleece top more snuggly around her, careful of the intravenous line leading into her chest. She made a mental note to wear warmer clothes next time. The throw Bethany had given her felt good, but her body seemed colder these days.

The older woman Jessie had met on her tour of the center—she thought her name was Irene—was settled back into one of the other recliners, covered from neck to toes with one of the blankets. *She must have grabbed one before they started her treatment*, Jessie thought. She'd try to remember to do that next time. The woman appeared to be asleep, but it was hard for Jessie to tell because of the gauze mask that covered her nose and mouth.

Settling back in her own chair, Jessie tried not to think of the poisons flowing into her vein. Somehow, she'd thought she would feel something, perhaps a burning sensation, but there was nothing. She could have been any woman sitting in a recliner watching television. Except for the IV pole and line.

A small, flat-screen TV was attached to the wall above the apartment-sized refrigerator. The channel was set to an oldies station, and Jessie didn't really care enough to change it. She sat through an episode of *In the Heat of the Night* before she dug her e-reader from her bag and tapped open the book she'd been reading. She tried her best, but it was hard to keep her mind on the novel. She felt strange to be lying back in a recliner in the middle of the morning. She couldn't get engrossed in the TV show, but neither could she focus on her book.

The woman in the corner recliner moved slightly, which Jessie found disconcerting. She hoped the woman was okay.

A young nurse in colorful scrubs came in twice to check the flow of the drugs on both Jessie's and Irene's stands. After making notes on a clipboard, she asked Jessie again if she'd care for a bottle of water or juice.

Jessie declined both, still unsure of what needing to go to the restroom would entail, but she appreciated the brief conversation with another person.

None of this felt real.

She pulled her cell phone from her tote bag and checked to see if Greg or Bethany had sent her a text message or a voice mail, wishing they had and being glad they hadn't at the same time. She knew what it was like. They'd get busy with details and tasks and phone calls, and the day would slip away. She tried to make herself understand. Still, she hoped she was at least on their minds, that they were thinking about her on some level. She fought against feeling sorry for herself, but she could envision both of them, the two people who were supposed to care about her the most, going on with their days, laughing with other people, making plans for lunch, and forgetting what day this was.

How often did your wife or your sister and best friend start chemotherapy? Jessie shook her head to dispel the gloomy thoughts. Life went on.

A quick glance at the clock over the window at the nurses' station showed one hour and fifteen minutes had passed.

Only another hour and forty-five minutes to go.

Chapter 13

Marcie hefted the basket of clean laundry onto her hip and made her way down the stairs. The floor plan had seemed ideal when they'd bought the house, with the kids basically having the entire upper level, leaving the main floor to the master suite, living room, office, and kitchen.

She knew the design of the house would be perfect in the future, but right now, she was tired of making the trip up and down the stairs several times each day—picking up dirty clothes and delivering clean clothes, helping to search for backpacks and library books, getting kids up, putting kids to bed. By the time the day was over, she was exhausted from just the sheer number of steps she had taken, all inside of their home.

She wasn't supposed to lift anything over ten pounds following her lumpectomy, but could a basket of laundry weigh anything close to that? She didn't think so, although after the third trip of the day, it felt that way.

How could life have changed so much in only a few weeks?

She remembered that pregnancy felt as if someone was draining energy from her body little by little, particularly during those last few weeks. This exhaustion was similar, except there would be no joy ahead of holding a newborn.

Once, when she had been ranting about the unfairness of all of this, Marc's comment had been, "You're just special."

The comment, she knew, had been said to make her feel better. Instead, it had irritated her, but she tried to put herself in Marc's place. While he hadn't been all that interested in the details, he'd been strong through the decisions they'd had to make following the devastating result from the MRI.

She had been smiling as she'd walked down the hallway in Dr. Catterson's office that day, savoring the compliments on her new boots from the two women in the waiting room. The smile had quickly disappeared.

"I'm sorry to give you bad news," Dr. Catterson had said. "But the lump is malignant."

The doctor had continued to explain the treatment options and what each entailed, but Marcie only remembered the walk back down the hallway and to her car. While she'd worked hard to think the lump hadn't been anything more than a pulled muscle, somewhere in the back of her mind, she had known better all along, and when she'd received the results from Dr. Catterson, it was almost a relief. She didn't have to work so hard to convince herself it was nothing. Knowing was freeing, in a way.

But they were just getting started. She had shared the news of her diagnosis, of her surgery, of what it had been like to start chemotherapy, with Lisa and Emily, of course. They'd been by her side through most of it, but the burden of helping her to maneuver the maze of decisions rested solely on Marc. He at least had flipped through the plastic file folder full of details about her treatment plan, definitions of chemicals, and anticipated side effects. Marcie suspected he just liked the challenge of trying to understand it all. Since being handed the folder on her first day of chemo, she had barely glanced at the pages. It was confusing and more than a little frightening.

"It's like being forced to learn a foreign language," she said to Marc. "And I don't even want to visit the country." He had laughed, and Marcie was glad to realize she still had some sense of humor.

Marcie dropped the basket of clothes by the washer and joined Marc on the leather sofa in the family room. The girls were upstairs, most likely watching a video. Christopher was having a sleep-over at a friend's, and the house was quiet. Marc put his arm around her, smoothing back her long hair and giving her a kiss on the back of her neck.

"You know, you don't have to understand everything in that folder," he said, motioning to the plastic binder on the coffee table. He knew her well. Marc enjoyed all of the latest technology—smartphones, tablets, iPads, and the countless applications that he studied nightly while watching TV. Marcie didn't understand how any of it worked, nor did she care.

"I just want my phone and computer to work. I don't need to know *how* they work," she often said. Marc's statement that she didn't have to study the contents of the plastic folder was a welcome permission slip to let others be in charge.

Marc's job as a sales rep for a national company kept him away from home for weeks at a time. Marcie took charge during those periods, but she always gladly turned the decisions over to Marc the minute he was home. Of course, the day-to-day decisions were hers to make by necessity, but she was happy to postpone any actions that could wait for her husband.

Marcie often had to remind herself that she had made important decisions on a daily basis when she worked as a public relations director for a nonprofit agency. She also had willingly given up her career to start a family. She didn't enjoy the weeks of separation while Marc was off on a job, but she had learned to deal with that aspect of their life. Most of her female friends thought it was ideal.

"How wonderful to be able to watch whatever you want on TV. Eat whatever you want, when you want," they would say wistfully.

Marcie suspected their attitudes were more about thinking the grass is always greener in someone else's backyard than really wishing their husbands had jobs that took them away from home. Marc's career afforded them a comfortable living, and she never worried about money. Still, she wished he could be at home more. She was always catching him up on the kids' activities, their latest interests, their latest dramas. She longed for a familiar routine instead of spending so much time apart and then trying to find their comfort zone again.

After her diagnosis, he'd suggested changing jobs. "I could find something else, something where I could be home every night."

"You'd hate that," Marcie had answered.

She had silently hoped he would actually do it, but he never brought up the idea again. Now, Marcie wondered if he would rather be somewhere else, anyplace where he could pretend life at home was going on as it had before. She wouldn't blame him if he did feel that way. After all, she felt that way a lot of the time.

Snuggled under an afghan, side by side on the sofa, Marc absently toyed with a strand of her hair, wrapping it around his fingers as they watched the movie.

Marcie was afraid to move, knowing it would spoil the moment, and Marc hadn't been particularly affectionate of late, but it bothered her to have his hands touching her hair. She hadn't lost a significant amount, but she knew it was thinning.

As if reading her mind, Marc dropped his hand to her shoulder, giving it a squeeze.

"You know, not everyone loses their hair," he said. "You might be one of the lucky ones who sails through chemo with no side effects."

Marcie reached up and took his hand, entwining her fingers with his. "I hope you're right," she said, "but you might have a big surprise the next time you're home."

He squeezed her fingers and leaned in until their heads touched but didn't react to her statement.

Chapter 14

"Are you kidding me? Good God!"

Jessie, along with all of the other female customers who had heard him, turned toward the voice. Greg was staring in amazement at the display of bras in the anchor store at the mall.

"Size F? My God." He continued his amazement at the bra sizes. Jessie mused that it was likely his first time in a lingerie department, and the experience was, literally, an eye-opener.

"In your dreams," she joked, sidling up to where he stood, apparently frozen, in front of a selection of enormous bras.

"More like in my nightmares. Those things could kill a guy." Greg gave a mock shudder and moved over to where Jessie was sorting through a display. "Find what you want?"

"Not yet. Dr. Catterson said I can't wear a bra with an underwire yet, and I don't really want another sports bra that gives me a uni-boob."

Greg shook his head, clearly out of his element. "Underwire? They put wire in bras? Doesn't that hurt?"

Jessie laughed. Shopping for bras had never been a pleasant experience, and while she felt like she needed something to give her new breasts a more natural look and feel, she hadn't been looking forward to this outing either. She'd also found it irritating, at least initially, that Greg had wanted to go with her. He had never helped her shop for bras in their twenty-eight years of marriage. But now that they were here, it was just funny and exactly what she had needed. The laughter felt good. Welcome. This was definitely a new experience for them both.

"An underwire gives more definition, but yeah, most are pretty uncomfortable," she explained to Greg, who nodded thoughtfully.

She continued to roam through the displays, fingering the flimsy materials as she passed.

"So what's a uni-boob?" Greg asked, seeming genuinely interested.

Jessie laughed again and shook her head. "Not a pretty sight unless you're running a marathon," she answered. "Sports bras can push your breasts together until you look like you just have one."

The other shoppers gave them a wide berth, several offering smiles and barely concealed laughter, while others openly gave them looks of disapproval. Those looks, Jessie noted, came mostly from women shopping the size F hangers.

Jessie actually felt sorry for those women with such large breasts. While they *might* be sexy in their twenties and thirties, they had to be back-breakers in their fifties. Or so she imagined. She'd never had experience in that department, and now she had even less.

She refused a clerk's offer to "fit" her. She had never accepted the offer in the past, and she certainly wasn't going to now. She thought of explaining that she'd had a mastectomy and wondered if the clerk had ever assisted someone who had had the surgery. Probably. Jessie knew there were bras made specifically for women after mastectomies, but to her, they just looked like padded bras with larger price tags.

She wandered through the racks, with Greg on her heels, and realized that she was happy to be shopping for a size B, even if it did need to be slightly padded. She could now be whatever size she wanted to be.

After selecting two bras, Jessie and Greg walked back through the mall, holding hands and checking out the clothing on mannequins. Both were in happy moods; the laughter from the lingerie department stayed with them. Greg pointed out different outfits that he thought would look great on Jessie, evidently forgetting that she wasn't a teenager.

"You are out of your mind," Jessie laughed, as Greg suggested a pair of barely there, body-hugging, fringed denim shorts.

The stores were starting to put out spring and summer merchandise. While Jessie enjoyed seeing the bright colors and new styles, she was drawn more to the racks of winter sales. It seemed that she was always cold these days. She picked out a soft orange zip-up sweatshirt and held it up for Greg to see. She wondered if he understood why she was suddenly favoring soft material and tops that were easy-on/easy-off.

"Cute," he said. "Ready to go?"

Jessie knew that was code for *Can we please get out of here?* She grinned at Greg as they stood in the checkout line.

This has been good, Jessie thought, squeezing her husband's hand.

She wondered briefly about the other women from the green room. Were they married? Were their husbands supportive? She couldn't imagine going through all of this without Greg by her side.

Before leaving the mall, they stopped in front of a Mexican restaurant.

"Let's have a drink. Chips and salsa too," Greg said, and Jessie smiled. He knew how much she loved Mexican food. He didn't care for it.

"Wonderful," she said. "This is so fun! Thanks."

"Thanks? For what?" Greg said. He looked quizzically at his wife.

Jessie felt tears suddenly welling in her eyes. She blinked quickly, not wanting to spoil the mood.

"Everything," she said, squeezing his hand.

The waiter brought their margaritas first, and Jessie had hers half drank by the time the chips and salsa arrived. As the driver, Greg was taking his time with the alcohol, but he dove into the chips.

"We didn't have any lunch," he said. "I just realized that. Want to order something more than chips?"

Jessie didn't reply. She could feel bile rising in her throat and sweat breaking out along her hairline. Greg's nearly full margarita spilled over as she pushed back from the table and ran to the restroom.

Crouched on the filthy floor, she vomited until her stomach was empty, and dry heaves took over. She felt weak and wasn't sure if she could stand without help.

A woman's voice came from outside the stall as she knocked timidly on the door. "Are you Jessie? Are you okay? Your husband asked me to check on you."

Now, tears ran down Jessie's face, and she choked back a sob. "I'm not sure if I can get up."

Thankfully, in her rush to make it to the toilet, Jessie hadn't locked the door. A woman who looked to be in her mid-sixties carefully pushed the door open. She leaned over Jessie and pushed the lever to flush the stool. She then took Jessie by the arm and helped her walk from the stall to the row of sinks.

Jessie was mortified. She wondered if Greg had told the woman that she was going through chemo. She wasn't sure if she hoped he had or hoped he hadn't.

"Better?" the woman asked.

Jessie fought the urge to collapse into her arms; she simply nodded instead, avoiding the woman's eyes. "I'm so embarrassed," she said. "Thank you so much."

The woman gave Jessie a sympathetic smile and then turned to leave. She looked quickly back before pushing open the door. "Watch out for those margaritas," she said and was gone.

Jessie looked at her reflection in the large mirror. Using a wet paper towel, she began to wipe the smeared mascara from under her eyes. She looked like hell and felt worse.

She wondered, but only for a second, if the nausea had come from drinking tequila on an empty stomach, or if it was a reaction to chemo. It was likely both, she knew. It was time to stop pretending that the treatments weren't going to change her.

Chapter 15

On day eighteen after her first chemo treatment, as Marcie showered, with eyes closed to keep the shampoo out, she realized her hands were full of hair. Standing under the hard stream of hot water, she ventured a look down and saw clumps of hair in her fingers. She tried to scrape off the strands, plastering them to the side of the shower stall, which was soon covered in swatches of her hair.

It wasn't going to stop coming out. She had to accept that. She stood with her forehead against a cool spot on the shower wall, tears streaming down her face. Wiping her eyes only made her cry more, as the tears mixed with strands of hair along her face and neck. It was gross, a nightmarish feeling. She dreaded stepping from behind the shower curtain to see herself in the mirror, but she also couldn't stay in the shower forever.

She had known this was coming. Right? At the very least, she had known it was a pretty strong possibility. She took a deep breath and then exhaled loudly. No big deal. Hair would grow back. She could do this.

She avoided looking in the mirror as she grabbed a towel off the bar and dried herself, blotting at her head as if to keep what hair was there attached. Then she saw that the towel too was covered in hair.

Grabbing a clean towel from the shelf, she quickly dried herself and pulled on a pair of black yoga pants and a long-sleeved T-shirt. She braved a quick glance at the mirror before leaving the bathroom, and the tears started again. The woman staring back looked like someone with a dreaded disease. AIDS, maybe. Marcie laughed sadly. She *was* a woman with a dreaded disease. Patches of pink scalp showed through fewer patches of dark hair. She grabbed the still-damp towel and quickly wrapped it around her head.

"Well, so much for thinking I might not lose my hair," she said aloud, trying not to sound as sad and frightened as she felt as she walked into the family room, where Marc sat in his recliner. Thankfully, the kids were still asleep. With the towel wrapped turban-style around her head, she hoped she didn't look as terrible as she feared she did.

"It's coming out?" he asked, looking up from where he was devouring the Sunday newspaper, laying sections aside as he finished with them and leaving the sports pages—his favorites—for last.

"Oh, yeah. By the handful," Marcie answered, trying to sound matter-of-fact, as if telling your husband that all of your hair is falling out was part of a normal conversation. "Guess I'll go ahead and clip off what's left. Should have done that already."

"Want me to do it?" Marc asked.

Marcie knew his offer was sincere. Even before she'd started chemo, he had offered to shave his own head as a show of support, but she had talked him out of it. It wouldn't have made her feel any better, and she also suspected he simply wanted to shave his head and that it had nothing to do with her. Plus, at that point, she'd still been hopeful that she'd be one of the lucky ones to keep her hair.

Marcie kept a hand on the towel, afraid it would slip off and expose her nearly bald head. She didn't want Marc to see that.

"Oh, I think I'd rather do it, but thanks," she said.

"Well, if you need help, just let me know," he replied, turning back to the newspaper.

She stood in the master bathroom, holding the clippers Marc used to trim his moustache. Carefully, she buzzed what was left of her hair to within a half inch of her tender pink scalp, the hair falling into the sink to mix with her tears.

Chapter 16

Jessie was feeling good. The apprehension that came with each appointment had diminished. At least she knew what to expect now—or hoped she did. If it didn't get any worse than this, she could deal with it. Other than the one episode at the mall after drinking that margarita, she hadn't vomited. Certain smells, including bacon grease, did make her queasy, but cutting pork from her diet was doable.

It did sting each time the needle was inserted into the port in her chest, and she strongly disliked every detail about the green room—the survivors' walk poster taped to the back of the screen, the skinny ivy that climbed up the wall and continued along the ceiling, the coffeepot that no one ever touched, the line of recliners—but the treatments themselves were bearable.

The e-reader proved to be a godsend. For one thing, she could play games or search the Internet when she grew tired of reading. She could also put in the earplugs to watch a movie—or to simply discourage conversation.

But it seemed the others who gathered in the small green room, with its black fake-leather recliners and companion IV stands, wanted to talk.

Karen and Irene seemed to be on the same schedule as Jessie. They saw each other every Thursday, usually sharing the entire three hours.

Karen worked at a local discount store, and she insisted that because of that, Jessie should recognize her. Jessie didn't.

"I've been there for almost ten years," Karen said, still trying to convince Jessie that she had to know her.

"I've probably seen you there, but I usually run in and out, always late for something," Jessie said, wanting to placate the woman and end the conversation.

It was clear Karen enjoyed her work. She talked about it incessantly and about the problems that she apparently solved single-handedly. She was fifty-one years old and married to a man named Jon. He stopped by the center one Thursday to bring Karen lunch, and Jessie had immediately escaped to her ear buds to remove herself from their conversation. She assumed the couple didn't have children, since Karen never mentioned any.

But Karen did seem to enjoy sharing news about how sick she had been, how horrible she felt every Thursday through Sunday, how nothing tasted right any more, and how wronged she felt to be diagnosed with cancer.

Jon had seemed nice and was friendly enough. He was a good balance to his wife's glass-half-empty personality.

Marcie, who was newer to the chemo room even than Jessie, mostly talked about her three children, all under the age of eight. They were apparently involved in a multitude of activities—soccer, dance, gymnastics, piano, crafts. Jessie enjoyed hearing her talk so animatedly about their hectic schedule, but she was also slightly intimidated by the younger woman. Marcie seemed to have it so together; Jessie usually felt as if she was hanging from a cliff by her fingertips, and with the slightest misstep, she would plummet into a dark hole.

Unlike the brief conversation they had shared at Dr. Catterson's office only weeks ago—mostly about Marcie's cute new boots—their time together during treatments gave them a better opportunity to know each other.

"We'd recently moved, and I'd helped carry in a zillion boxes," Marcie told the women. "I found a lump in the shower the first morning in our new house and thought I'd just pulled a muscle or something. No such luck."

If any of us has the right to feel indignant about our diagnoses, it should be Marcie, Jessie thought. And maybe she did feel wronged. Jessie thought there was something reserved about the young woman, and she wondered if it might have more to do with Marcie's husband than her cancer. Jessie noticed that Marcie mentioned Marc only in connection to the children. None of the women had ever seen him. Of course, they hadn't met Greg either, so maybe she was just imagining things.

Irene never spoke. She stayed hidden behind her white mask. Jessie sensed that she listened to their conversations, though, and would sometimes feel that the older woman was smiling at something that had been said. She wondered what Irene's story was. She was usually already there and settled back in a black recliner when Jessie came in for treatments. And Irene was usually still in the recliner when Jessie finished. Could her treatments be longer than three hours? *Good Lord*, Jessie thought.

She was always sure to smile at Irene when she settled in each Thursday morning. It seemed to Jessie that Irene always smiled back, judging from the way her skin crinkled at the corners of her eyes at the sides of her gauze mask. But she never spoke. No one ever came to sit with her, though Jessie understood that didn't necessarily mean Irene didn't have family and friends. No one came to be with Jessie either, at her own request.

Other patients occasionally ended up in the green room at the same time as those Jessie called the "regulars." Sometimes, others would be there because of a scheduling change or because blood work had shown their bodies weren't adapting to the harsh drugs. It was unusual, though, for a man to be in the treatment center at the same time as the women. Jessie wondered if that was by design, to allow the women privacy. *It's not necessary*, she thought. *There's nothing private about cancer.* And it was refreshing when a man did show up.

One of those men was Jim, a sixty-five-year-old farmer. In his worn blue jeans and plaid shirt, with an obvious farmer's tan, he had a simple, open way about him that Jessie enjoyed.

"I know your husband," he said by way of introduction. "I was one of his first customers—if not *the* first customer—he had when he opened the business."

"Really?" Jessie grinned at him as they both settled into their respective recliners. It was nice to have a new topic of conversation. "That was a long time ago."

"It was," Jim said, smiling at the memory. "He was a young kid then. Before you ever entered the picture, I think. Nice guy."

"Still is." Jessie smiled back.

She looked forward to sharing the conversation with Greg. They had a standing joke that wherever they happened to go, whether it was out to dinner, to the movies, at a ballgame, or attending a boat show—the odds were good that they'd run in to someone who knew him. Casual conversation came easily for Greg, and he made friends wherever they went.

She knew Greg would enjoy hearing about her meeting with Jim, even though she wished they had met somewhere else. She watched as the nurse started his IV, lightly touching his shoulder as she moved on to check the status of Jessie's infusion.

"Prostate," Jim said. His smile had disappeared, replaced by a look of concern. "You?"

Jessie smiled at him, thinking this wasn't a conversation they would be having in any other setting. "Breast," she answered, surprised that she didn't feel self-conscious about saying the word.

Jim shifted in his recliner, searching for a comfortable spot. "I've only had one chemo dose," he said. "This will be my second. Dr. Park is having trouble coming up with a drug mix that my body will tolerate. I was sicker than a dog after the first treatment. My blood counts are all over the place. Guess we'll see how I do today."

"Well, good luck," Jessie said, not knowing an appropriate response. "Hopefully, you'll do okay with this one." She turned back to her book.

A woman Jessie supposed was Jim's wife took a seat beside him, offering Jessie a tentative smile before opening a magazine.

When Greg got home from work that night, Jessie told him about meeting Jim and his comment about being one of Greg's first customers.

"He said you were a nice guy," Jessie said, grinning at her husband.

Greg laughed at his memory of Jim. "He was the nice guy. I was so green at the job. I had no idea what I was doing. I think Jim knew that and placed an order just to be kind. He's a good guy."

Jessie never saw Jim again. A few months later, she learned more about his life and his family, about his military service, his involvement in the community, and his hobbies as she read his obituary. Yes, a nice guy. She was glad to have met him.

And the fact of his death shook her to her core.

In dealing with chemo and its aftereffects—sleeping most of the day on Fridays, Saturdays, and Sundays and then rushing to catch up on work, laundry, shopping, and cooking before the next Thursday came—she had almost forgotten what this was all about. She was fighting a disease that could kill.

Chapter 17

For her third chemo treatment, Jessie donned the shaggy, highlighted wig that her sister had talked her into buying. It was cute, and if she admitted it, it was actually more stylish than her real hair. She had splurged on it, the first of her many moments in the last few months of thinking, *I deserve this!*

She remembered Bethany's urging her to buy a wig in the first few days after her diagnosis. Thank heavens she had. It would have been horrible to shop for one with a bald head. It was bad enough as it was.

They had been shopping for the boots that Bethany thought she absolutely had to have and were driving to a convenience store to buy soft drinks for the trip home when Beth had suddenly swerved into a strip mall.

"Where are we going?" Jessie had asked and then noticed the hair salon located in the middle of the shops, with a sign in the window advertising wigs. She had felt immediate panic.

"Oh, Bethany. I don't want to do this now. Really, I don't."

Her sister had just grinned. "No time like the present. Come on; it'll be fun." And she was out of the car and entering the shop before Jessie could argue.

The salon was a busy place. Women sat in chairs in different stages of styling, some with their hair clipped into odd formations for cuts and others with shiny foil wrapped around their hair for highlights.

A stylist looked up from her work and smiled. "How can I help you?"

"We're shopping for a wig," Bethany answered, brightly, smiling back at Jessie, who stood just inside the front door, looking as if she wanted to bolt.

The woman took them to the lower level of the shop, where an assortment of wigs in all lengths, colors, and styles sat atop Styrofoam heads. Two dressers, topped with small mirrors, were located at the back of the room.

"Let me finish with my customer, and I'll come help you," the stylist said. "But help yourself. Try some on. See what you like." She walked back up the stairs, leaving Jessie and Bethany alone.

"I don't want to do this," Jessie said again. Her voice was small and frightened.

"You don't have to buy one today," Bethany said, moving forward to take a wig off its stand. She gave Jessie a soft smile. "Let's just get an idea of what you'll want. Just try some on. Come on. I'll try one on, too."

Bethany sat down quickly in one of the dresser chairs, yanking her own hair back and pulling on a long, black wig. "What do you think? Am I rocking this look or what?"

Jessie had to laugh. Bethany had always been the stronger one. She seemed to know the right thing to say, the right thing to do, and what her little sister needed.

"I don't really think that's your look," Jessie answered, forcing herself to smile at Bethany's reflection in the mirror.

Bethany pulled off the wig to try on a curly blonde one. "Well, that's the idea, little sister. This is your chance to try something totally new. Have any look you want." She picked up the black wig she had just pulled off and handed it to Jessie. "Just try it on. For me."

Jessie sat down at the adjacent vanity and glanced in the mirror. She looked tired. She really didn't want to do this. But she pulled the wig on anyway, forcing a smile. "I just need some fishnet stockings, and I can go as Cher for Halloween," she said, trying to match Bethany's mood but failing. Tears started flowing just as the stylist came back down the stairs.

"Find anything that you—" She stopped midsentence when she noticed Jessie's tear-stained face. "Oh, honey," she said, wrapping her arms around Jessie. "Are you going through chemo?"

Jessie nodded. "How did you know?"

The older woman pulled back just enough to look into Jessie's eyes. "I've been there too," she answered.

In the end, Jessie decided on the shaggy, highlighted wig. Not so different from her own hair but thicker.

The stylist urged her to buy a synthetic wig, rather than one of human hair. "With human hair . . . well, it's human hair," the woman had explained. "You still have to wash it, dry it, style it, spray it—everything you do now. Trust me; you won't want to do that. Buy synthetic, and all you have to do is shampoo it occasionally, give it a good shake, and it will fall back into place."

Bethany had said that made sense, and the two women approved of Jessie's choice.

The wig cost two hundred dollars, but, as Bethany had pointed out, Jessie would save that much—probably more—by not having hair appointments during the next year or so.

"Plus," Bethany said, "you may want to wear the wig in the future, even after your hair comes back."

Jessie doubted that.

But she was thankful Beth had talked her into getting the wig. Since the morning her real hair had fallen out, on day fifteen after starting chemo, she'd mostly worn a soft knit cap. The cap was more comfortable than the wig, but she didn't like wearing it outside of the house. While some women could pull off wearing scarves, hats, or ball caps, she wasn't one of them. The wig was well made and actually did flatter her.

Still, she always worried that it wasn't exactly where it was supposed to be on her head, or worse, that it might fall off. She tried to avoid pulling on the ear flaps in public, knowing the move was a dead giveaway.

She remembered Pam adjusting her own wig the day they had met in the green room. Jessie hadn't known it was a wig until she'd done that.

The wig was always slightly off-kilter after Jessie's hours in the recliner, but then she just went back home anyway. The treatments didn't hurt, but they were tiring.

For Jessie, it was the sitting—the simple act of sitting—for three hours that was exhausting. She wondered if there had been any time in her past when she had ever sat in one spot for that length of time. During college? Maybe, although she didn't think she'd ever taken any class that had been that long. She tried not to think about what was being put into her body. Even though she knew the chemicals were supposed to attack any errant cancer cells roaming through her system after the surgery, she'd been told they also would attack and destroy some healthy cells in the process.

"Seems like overkill," Jessie had confessed to Greg.

She had felt fine after the first two treatments, and she expected to feel fine after this one too. Between watching several TV shows, reading for a while, and connecting to the Wi-Fi in the green room to download and watch a movie, the hours had actually gone by quickly. She'd crawled back into bed and taken a nap after returning home and was up cooking dinner by the time Greg came through the door after work.

"You feel okay?" he asked, as he had after every treatment. He had offered to go with her to each of them, but really, she didn't want to worry about him for three hours. A person can flip through only so many old magazines, and he wasn't one to read a book or to watch TV for that long. Well, he would for a basketball game, but there weren't any sports programs on weekday mornings.

Besides, she *did* feel okay. In fact, she had more energy than she'd had in the weeks before starting chemotherapy, when worry and anticipation had worn her down. She liked to think that the process of healing was now in action.

Jessie still stood on the deck in the early morning hours of each day, and she recited her mantra: "I'm healthy. I'm healing. I'm happy, and I'm strong." The words seemed to help convince her that all of those things were true. If she happened to be up early enough to catch her stars before they disappeared into the day, she felt even stronger.

She remembered Pam's words on that first day, telling her that the weeks of chemo would go fast. Jessie wasn't sure she agreed. She hated planning her life around treatments and doctor appointments.

Her green-room friends seemed to be doing well. They shared conversations about their jobs, their families, what they were cooking for dinner that night, their kids, their favorite television shows and movies—and the changes in their bodies.

Jessie was getting to know each of them a little better. Their conversations gave her an idea about what was most important to them, what aspects of their lives helped get them through all of this. Their shared forced confinement in the black recliners, hour after hour, had created an understanding and appreciation for each other. Jessie was a bit surprised by this sense of camaraderie, and she wondered if the others were as well.

Other than cancer, they had little in common. Evidently, it was enough.

Three weeks down.

Chapter 18

Pam sat tall on the barstool at her kitchen counter. The smell of the hair dye in the little plastic bowl beside her seemed too strong. She had opened the French doors to the patio, but the fresh air couldn't dilute the fumes. If anything, the air coming in made them stronger.

"Are you sure you mixed that right? It smells terrible."

A friend, Tricia, was dyeing Pam's hair for the second time since she'd finished treatments. Her naturally blonde hair had come in white and coarser than it had been before chemo. They both were hoping the color would cover better this time.

"It's mixed right," Tricia said. "Maybe your sense of smell is heightened."

Pam laughed and wondered if Tricia might be right. When she had finally summoned up the nerve to ask Dr. Park if it was okay to dye her hair, she'd been relieved to see him smile.

"It's fine," Dr. Park had answered. "You know, I probably get asked that question more than anything. Women always want to know, as soon as their hair comes back in, if it's okay to dye it. It's not going to hurt you, and if it makes you feel better, by all means do it."

Pam had seen Internet blogs that warned women who had undergone treatment for breast cancer against using hair color, but considering the toxins that had been pumped into her system over the course of six weeks, she thought a little dye on the scalp was nothing. Besides, it just felt fun to be doing this again. She had been dyeing her hair, one color or another, since high school.

She was eager to show the women in the "green room," as they had come to call the treatment center, her new 'do. As the one in the group who was now finished with chemo and only showed up for blood work and booster shots, Pam knew they looked to her for hope that their lives too would be normal again someday. Yes, it was a "new normal" (God, she hated that term) but still more normal than what their lives entailed now. When she'd been new to the green room, she too had clung to any news of others who had finished with treatments and were going on about their lives. Now, she was that person.

"Okay, thirty minutes and we'll rinse you off," Tricia said, gathering up the bottle of color, conditioner, and the empty box and poking the plastic gloves in on top of it all.

"Shouldn't you keep out the gloves?" Pam asked.

"Nah, you can just jump in the shower and rinse it off in there."

Grabbing their coffee mugs, Pam and Tricia made their way onto the patio to wait for the kitchen timer to ring. Settling into the comfortable patio chair, Pam breathed in the cool, crisp air and turned her face up to the warmth of the sun. She didn't know if she was naturally enjoying the simpler things in life or mentally forcing herself to take a minute to acknowledge them. *Does it matter?* she thought. Maybe living in the moment took consciousness to achieve. Whatever the reason, she was learning to savor every second.

"You should have had some of the women from the center over today," Tricia said, watching her friend sit in the sunshine with her eyes closed.

Pam didn't answer.

"They might have gotten a kick out of watching us dye your hair," Tricia continued. "You know, encouragement for when they get to this point."

Pam knew Tricia meant well. Pam had told her about the other women in the green room and had even entertained the thought of doing just that, making this morning a hair-coloring party. Without delving too deeply into the thought, she knew she wasn't in the mood to have any of them over. Karen, she was sure, would have been a downer. She seemed to find the negative whenever she could. Marcie likely had errands to run with her young children. Plus, she was so young and cute that Pam felt a little ancient around her. Jessie would have been the only one she'd considered inviting, but she wasn't sure that was the right thing to do either. According to updates from the chemo nurses, Jessie had just lost her hair. She doubted that she would want to come. She didn't really know that much about her, although it had seemed as if they had connected and that they could be friends. She hoped so.

"Maybe next time," Pam said. She could have explained to Tricia that the other women were behind her in treatments and that they were still dealing with the reality of being bald. But she didn't think her friend would understand.

And besides, they were "treatment friends." Inviting them into her life outside of the controlled environment of the green room would change the dynamics, and it wasn't a change that Pam was sure she wanted. Could lasting friendships be founded on mutual health issues? She wasn't sure about that. Maybe.

Away from the green room, life was normal—to some degree at least. Pam could go hours without thinking about her disease. She could forget her diagnosis. She could forget that people were being diagnosed with cancer right now. She could set aside the knowledge of what they had to go through to fight it and of what she had gone through.

She had only finished chemo a few weeks ago, and already it seemed in the distant past. She still went to her daily radiation treatments, but they were quick, and because someone always had to drive her there and back, the days took on a semblance of "outings," with lunch and shopping afterwards. She actually wondered if she'd miss these days once the six weeks were completed.

Here, on her patio with Tricia, she could imagine that life was as it had always been "before." She hated having an event in life that categorized happenings. There were things that came before and after Stephen's death. There were the things that came before and after her diagnosis. She just wanted a seamless life without divisions.

She didn't think Tricia would understand, and she really didn't feel like trying to explain it. What Tricia did seem to get was that this event of coloring her hair was just that: an event. Pam appreciated that.

As if reading her mind, Tricia stood up from the wrought-iron table. "We need something stronger," she said, heading to the kitchen. "Got wine?"

Pam laughed. "I think so. On the side door of the refrigerator. Should be good and aged. Who knows how long that bottle has been there? I hope it's not vinegar by now."

Pam turned her gaze to the backyard. The yard was one of the reasons she and Stephen had bought the house. Oh, not the only reason. She had loved the massive brick and stone Tudor-style home on first sight. The four bedrooms and three baths were a plus when the kids came home, but it was the backyard, with its mass of trees and tangled, overgrown vines, that was the main appeal. When they had moved in, it had seemed like a wilderness in the midst of suburbia. Stephen's kids had loved it. She could see them in her memory now, climbing onto the tire swing Stephen had hung from a massive tree in one corner, screaming and arguing about taking turns. Adam had been thirteen; Anne, eleven.

Putting in a pool had gobbled up much of the yard, but it had been worth it. The pool had been the centerpiece of numerous parties, celebrations of birthdays, last days of school, and finally, graduations. She and girlfriends had great conversations while sunning beside the pool. Now, she rarely used it. She didn't know if chlorinated water was harmful, considering the port in her chest, and sunbathing wasn't a good idea for anyone, let alone someone fighting cancer. Another reason was that a swimsuit hadn't been invented that was flattering to her new body shape. The lack of breasts, or at least real ones, was the least of it. The lack of any strenuous exercise for the past year had left her body flabby. *I'll work on that*, she thought, *and soon*.

Now, the tire swing was still, as the kids were young adults and out on their own. Adam and Anne were still finding their way into careers and relationships. They still visited occasionally, and Pam enjoyed the times they did, but those were growing more infrequent. They called—or more accurately, texted—more often now. But that was okay.

She was glad they didn't seem to be overly attached to the house, because she probably wouldn't be living in it much longer. Her health insurance had paid the bulk of the big expenses for surgeries, treatments, and drugs, but her deductible was high enough that the disease had still taken a considerable toll on her bank account.

The other women in the green room thought she was their strength, their proof that everything would be okay. *They are wrong*, Pam thought. *It's knowing I need to be strong for them, or at least appear to be strong, that gives me strength*.

"Are you listening for the timer?" Tricia asked, interrupting Pam's thoughts as she returned with the bottle of wine. "We don't want to get drunk and ignore it, or you'll end up with fried hair."

Pam shook away the dismal thoughts about her financial situation and grinned at Tricia, rolling her eyes. "I already have fried hair, remember? Can't do much about that. It's the white that I hate."

Both relaxed back into their chairs in the sunlight, ready to enjoy their glasses of wine.

Chapter 19

Jessie was enjoying the warm sun and her unexpected "date" with Greg, who had grinned from ear to ear when she agreed to go to the lake with him. Though the air was chilly, and it was too early in the season for boating, she knew how excited he was to go. He had bought the ski boat on sale in the fall and had been eager to get it on water. It was a gorgeous day, and the lake was still and deep blue. No other boats were out, which Jessie chalked up to their owners having more sense than to be on the water at this time of year.

Jessie had wrapped a colorful scarf over her head, as much to keep the wig on as to keep the chilled wind away from her ears. She had considered wearing a ball cap over the wig but decided that a scarf lessened the chance of the wig going anywhere.

Greg didn't know why she worried about the baldness so much. "Just let people wonder," he said. "Be comfortable, and don't worry about what anyone else thinks. I mean, look at what all you've been through,"

That was just it. She didn't worry about what others would think; she did worry about what *she* thought. Having hair, albeit it a wig, made her feel better about herself, as if she was just any woman and not one who was sick. Besides, Greg hadn't seen her bald. She wore the wig until changing into pajamas at night, when she put on a pink knit cap, a gift Bethany had secretly purchased at the wig shop while Jessie wasn't watching.

Both the wig and the knit cap would soon be too warm to be comfortable, but that was a few months off. She knew how 1960s she looked when she added a colorful scarf to the 'do whenever it was windy or rainy. *Oh, well*, she thought. A dated scarf-around-the-head look was better than her "hair" blowing off. And that would be a very real possibility as spring and summer weather moved in, bringing more wind to the region.

She was as ready as Greg to be doing something exciting, something different from the normal day. Greg started the motor, and the craft moved easily away from the dock. Soon, they were gliding through the waves that glistened in the afternoon sun.

It took only a moment for Jessie to realize the scarf was too long. The breeze created by the speeding boat whipped it into her eyes. Still not confident the scarf would hold the wig in place, she kept one hand on top of her head.

Rushing the season, she had opted for a thin cotton shirt and a pair of jeans, both of which no longer fit. The shirt was too loose with her now-smaller breasts and the cold air off the lake blew through the top, chilling her. The jeans were too tight, due to weight gain from the daily steroids she took in the effort to avoid nausea. She was uncomfortable and knew she probably looked ridiculous, with the flowing scarf blowing around her head.

In spite of the discomfort, Jessie was elated to be out on a lake, in a boat, with her husband, doing something normal and fun. The sunshine felt good, and the occasional splashes of lake water that sprayed her arms and face were cold but refreshing.

Greg turned the boat, which was now soaring over the wave tops and then crashing down upon them. Queasiness hit Jessie immediately, as each thudding motion of the boat sent flashes of pain through her armpits. Jessie could feel a pull on the scars across both breasts. She fought to keep from vomiting.

"You okay?" Greg suddenly looked as frightened as Jessie felt. He cut the motor, and the boat slowed immediately. "Your face went completely white. Are you all right?"

At once, Jessie hated the look of concern in his eyes. "No. I'm not all right," she cried, her voice quaking. "I can't do this. I feel sick, and I hurt. You have to take me back."

The moment the words were out of her mouth, she wished she hadn't said them. But she *was* sick, and she *did* hurt, and she was so angry and so tired of the whole thing. Sick and tired of it. The discomfort, the constant worry that everything inside of her was wrong, the trying too hard to act like everything was okay. With everyone. She had wanted to forget all of it for just one afternoon, to laugh, to have fun. It wasn't fun any longer. Not for either of them.

They made their way back to the dock in silence, and Jessie walked up the steep bank while Greg secured the boat.

"Wait a minute. I'll walk up with you," he said.

Jessie felt embarrassed for some reason. She kept walking faster so that she would stay ahead of her husband. She didn't know who she was any more.

She stood at the top of the boat ramp, unsure of what to do next. She wanted to get out of the stupid shirt and uncomfortable jeans, for starters. But she didn't have any other clothes with her, just a jacket. She grabbed it from the Jeep, pulled it tight around her, and started walking down the road. She didn't know where she was going, but she didn't want to see Greg right now—or for him to see her.

Before she could gain any composure, Greg was at the top of the hill and walking quickly toward her. He grabbed her by the waist and wrapped his arms tightly around her.

"Jess, it's okay," he said. "It was just too soon. That's all."

She spun around to face him, breaking his embrace. "It is not okay, Greg," she said, flinging his words back at him in anger. "Nothing is okay." She hated feeling justified at the sudden fear in his eyes. "Everyone keeps telling me that I'm doing great, that everything is going to be okay. Well, guess what? I'm not doing great. I'm not okay."

He took a step toward her. "Jess . . ."

"No," she said, stepping away from his reach. "Oh, I'm great . . . in the green room. Everyone says so: the nurses, the cardiologist, Dr. Park, Dr Ames. I'm just great there. I'm great when I sleep all day—for most of every week. I'm a good little cancer patient. But I take a normal boat ride, a simple boat ride, and you see what happens."

Who was she kidding? She wasn't great at all.

They rode home in silence. When Greg reached his hand across the seat toward her, Jessie pretended not to see it. She knew fear was again masquerading as anger, but of the two emotions, she preferred anger.

Chapter 20

Jessie saw Pam only on shot days, when chemo patients got a weekly inoculation to boost their blood counts, particularly the white cells that would help fight infection. It was a constant threat, since their immune systems were compromised.

Jessie was always pleased and inspired to see the first "friend" she had met in the green room, knowing Pam was about two months ahead of her in the process. She considered it a lucky day when their appointments coincided. She gauged what her own future would hold by how well Pam was doing, and Pam always seemed to be doing great.

"Your hair is darling," Pam said, smiling at Jessie. "So glad you had the wig when you needed it. It looks great on you." She ran her hands through the short spikes of blonde hair that framed her pale face, asking, "What do you think of my new look?"

It wasn't a style that anyone (not anyone Jessie knew, anyway) would have asked for from a hairdresser. But for those who knew the reality of looking into a mirror and seeing a bald head, it was awesome. It was hair.

"Cute, cute," Jessie answered. "Is that your natural color?"

Jessie had grown to appreciate hair stories. Everyone passed along the fact that when—not if—your hair returned, it could be totally different: darker, lighter, straighter, thicker, curly, straight. *Growing back with highlights is not likely*, Jess thought, smiling to herself. She had worn her hair highlighted for so many years that she was no longer sure of her natural color. She was curious to see what appeared on her scalp when her hair did start to come back.

"No, not even close," Pam answered, laughing. She fluffed the short strands of hair with her fingers.

She looks like a punk rocker, Jessie thought, and it fit her upbeat personality.

"My natural color is mousy brown, but it came in totally white, and it was never straight, but it sure is now. A friend colored it for me, but we probably left the dye on too long. It was a little scary to see what it was going to look like when I rinsed it off, but I like it. A little more blonde that I wanted, but it's okay." Pam smiled at Jessie in her recliner. "How much longer?"

"Three more," Jessie answered, smiling at what was likely the longest conversation she'd ever had about hair. Three was such a little number, and she was glad to be able to say that. "Any tricks to making your hair grow back in quicker?"

"Eye-makeup remover." Pam grinned.

"Seriously?"

"Well, I think it helped. I felt like my eyelashes and eyebrows came back pretty quickly. Even though there wasn't anything there, I still used makeup to make it look like I had lashes and brows. And I always used the remover before I went to bed. One day I just decided to put it on my head too, to see what would happen. I don't know if it really helped, but it seemed like it did."

Jessie made a mental note to add eye-makeup remover to her drugstore list, along with vitamin D. An Internet blog by a woman who had gone through chemo said she was convinced that the vitamin had helped speed up the return of her hair. It was worth a try. Jessie was eager to tell the other women in the green room about the eye-makeup remover.

The women shared tips on dealing with breast cancer, collected from books, pamphlets, talk shows, and magazines but mostly from websites. There was no shortage of sites devoted to everything and anything, from whether you should or shouldn't shave your legs while going through chemo to renewing your sexual relationship after breast surgery.

While the group laughed about many of the posts, Jessie knew that they clung to some of the answers like lifelines, as she did. These were more than survival tips; this was valuable knowledge that there were women out there in cyberspace who had made it through all of this, despite the statistics that showed some of them wouldn't.

Pam was on her way out of the center and stopped to visit for a few minutes with Karen and Marcie, who were finishing up with their weekly treatments. She also stopped by to say hello to Irene before she waved good-bye to the group and pushed open the heavy door.

Jessie unzipped her fleece top enough so that the nurse could access the port, and she noticed Marcie watching her. "I bet the nurses think this is the only top I have," Jessie said, laughing. "It's what I always wear because it's soft on my incisions and easy to zip open."

"I was just thinking that it is perfect. I need to get something like that," Marcie said. "It hides a lot, too." As if suddenly realizing she might have said something insulting, Marcie hastily apologized. "I just mean you can't tell anything, you know? Oh, God. I'm making it worse. Sorry."

Marcie felt such a bond with the other women in the green room. They had taken her under their wings; she would never have guessed how much she would appreciate their concern for her. The shock of being diagnosed with breast cancer at the age of thirty-four was eased somewhat by her appreciation of being the "baby" of the group. Pam, Jessie, and even Karen treated her like a little sister, and she savored their outpouring of concern and attitude of protection. Her chosen recliner was adjacent to Irene's, and although the older woman never spoke, she had taken on the role of caring grandmother in Marcie's mind. She was always there.

Now, Marcie felt horrible that she might have hurt Jessie's feelings.

"No problem," Jessie said, laughing to put the younger woman at ease. "I knew what you meant. It's bulky enough that you can't tell I don't have anything under it. Bra or anything else."

They were the only two in the green room at that moment, and Jessie could sense the younger woman's discomfort. *Or maybe*, Jessie thought, *she needs to talk*.

"I've had this top for ages, and it's getting pretty worn, but you're right. It's comfortable," Jessie said. She smiled at Marcie, startled again at seeing someone so young going through all of this.

Marcie smiled back and then asked, "What surgery did you have?"

It was a question that anyone not going through this would hesitate to ask, but Jessie understood. The rules were different here.

"Double mastectomy," Jessie answered. "I had lumps in both breasts, so it made sense for me." She avoided use of the words cancer or malignancy. Obviously, that was a given. "You?"

"Lumpectomy," Marcie answered, "but I've had some complications, so I may end up having a mastectomy after all. I might be a candidate for the flap. I don't know."

The flap, Jessie had learned prior to her own surgery, entailed bringing tissue around from the back or up from the abdomen to form a new breast. Pretty radical, it seemed to her, but for some women, it was the best choice. And some doctors preferred it, she had read, since the newly formed breast would be from the woman's own tissue, rather than artificial material.

Marcie shrugged, attempting to mask what Jessie knew was fear and a feeling of losing any semblance of control. She could tell that the young woman was on the verge of tears. There was no point in offering platitudes. She could say that yes, it was truly amazing what surgeons could now do, and yes, it would probably all be okay in the long run. But none of them knew that. Still, they were lucky that medical science had come as far as it had in their lifetimes. Lucky? Well, everything was relative. They were luckier than women diagnosed with breast cancer only a decade ago.

Instead, she offered Marcie a warm smile and settled back in the recliner. She hoped the smile conveyed how much she cared.

Marcie followed the nurse down the hallway to have her blood drawn and vital signs taken, a weekly ritual for them all.

Jessie looked around the room and smiled at Irene, who was in her usual spot, covered with a white blanket and wearing her mask and knit cap. From a change in the older women's eyes, Jessie surmised that Irene had smiled back. She wondered if Irene's cancer was advanced. More than the others who frequented the green room, Irene took extra precautions. Nearly continual use of antibacterial hand cleanser was common, but Irene was the only person Jessie had met who wore a mask during treatment sessions. Jessie wondered again if she wore it to avoid contamination or to avoid conversation.

The desire to remain private in a mostly nonprivate atmosphere was certainly understandable, and Jessie knew that sometimes a simple conversation was too much of an effort.

It was nice to have just the two of them in the room. The quiet was comforting.

Greg still offered, occasionally, to accompany Jessie to her treatments, but she continued to decline.

"I'm just going to be sitting there, reading or watching TV. There's no reason for you to be there, and you'd be bored out of your mind," she told him.

Still, she had occasional twinges of jealousy when Jon offered to make a deli run for Karen. So far, he had been the only husband to show up during their treatments. Jessie had a fleeting thought that maybe all of Karen's griping was a good thing; it got her husband here. But solitude was okay. Greg wasn't there physically, but she knew he stood beside her.

Early in the process, she had sent him a text message when her treatment was over: "Done. Yay."

He had answered, "Done with what?"

She had passed it off as knowing he was busy at work, or maybe he was joking, but still it hurt. She hadn't wanted breast cancer, chemotherapy treatments, or surgeries to define her or her life, but, unfortunately, they mostly did. She understood, and in some measure appreciated, that Greg wasn't constantly thinking of her in that regard or dwelling on the image of her sitting in a black recliner with an IV pole beside it and a tube running into her chest. But still, his occasional seeming indifference hurt.

Jessie knew that some people going through treatments also went through counseling to help them deal with the changes in their lives. She didn't want to do that, but she could understand it. It was like the stages of grief: denial, anger, bargaining with God, depression and, eventually, acceptance. She'd gone through all of those steps, forward and backward and then revisited them out of order.

Much like grieving the loss of a loved one, it was tough losing life as you knew it, as you expected it to be, along with parts of your body. And while friends and family certainly didn't intend to make it any tougher, they often did. Casual comments made to a grieving person could take on enormous proportions. The same was true with other life-changing events, such as cancer.

One morning, a nurse stopped Jessie in the hallway. She wasn't one of Jessie's nurses, but they'd known each other casually for years, outside of any medical connection.

"I heard you have breast cancer," the woman said. "How are you?"

Jessie appreciated the lack of pity in her voice, which she knew was likely due to her medical training, but the tone sounded just a little more curious than Jessie felt was comfortable.

"Doing great," she had answered, forcing herself to be cheerful. "Anxious to be done with everything."

The nurse had cocked her head to one side and studied Jessie's face. "Well, you look great. You really do. I had heard you weren't doing well, but you look good."

The comment was like a slap, but Jessie refused to let the woman see that it had rattled her.

"Really?" she replied. "Who told you I wasn't doing well?"

The nurse/acquaintance muttered something about not remembering where she had heard that, said she was glad Jessie was doing okay, and hurried away.

The comment stayed with Jessie. While she was telling everyone she was doing great and working hard to believe it, were people gossiping that she was on her deathbed? And if so, why? Did they know something she didn't? Did she look worse than she thought?

She told Bethany about the conversation, fighting tears and pleading for honesty. "Tell me the truth. Do I look sick? Different?"

"Honesty?" her sister had echoed. "I'll give you honesty. That woman is an idiot. No, worse than an idiot. Whatever that might be. You are doing great. You look great. You truly do. And you know that, Jess! I think she's probably just jealous."

They had both laughed, and Jessie could feel the stress easing.

"Yeah, she's just jealous. That's it; I'm sure," Jessie had said, laughing away the tears. But the remembered comment still stung.

Chapter 21

"My fingers are as big as sausages," Karen announced the following Thursday, spreading her hands out for the others in the green room to see. "I'm glad I stopped wearing my rings before all of this happened. I would never have been able to get them off otherwise."

"Maybe you've got sausage fingers, but look at my moon-pie face," Marcie said, blowing out her cheeks to make her face even more round. She wore a colorful scarf around her head.

Jessie wondered briefly if Marcie had lost her hair, but she hadn't said anything so hopefully not.

The women in the green room laughed at the young woman's antics.

"Sausage fingers and moon pies. We're yummy," Marcie said, enjoying her place in the camaraderie. As the youngest, she brought a strong dose of reality to the situation and mostly delivered it with humor.

From her recliner in a corner, it was evident that Irene also thought the comment was funny. The sides of her mask quivered; her eyes shone bright above it.

Karen disregarded the comments from the others, and Jessie suspected that she hadn't liked the attention being diverted from her. In Karen's view, this—all of this—was about only her.

"I've lost weight everywhere but my fingers. They're always swollen," Karen said, disregarding Marcie's attempt to lighten the mood. "I'm getting downright skinny. My clothes don't even fit anymore. My husband still thinks I look great, though, so that's something. I tell him he's crazy, but he only says he's crazy in love."

In Jessie's experience, anyone who professed to be "crazy in love" was pretty much, well, just crazy. The thought was mean, she knew, but she just didn't seem to be able to help herself when it came to Karen. Even when the woman was trying to be upbeat, it came off as negative.

"I hate for him to see me here," Karen continued, waving her hands to take in the room. "He shouldn't have to go through this. It's bad enough that I have to."

Jessie let the comment pass, mostly because she couldn't come up with a quick answer to Karen's words but also because not wanting spouses in the green room was an understood feeling. It was a different atmosphere for the other women when Jon was there, as he flipped through old copies of *Sports Illustrated* and checked his watch every two minutes.

Maybe it was only Jessie's mood, but it seemed to her as if Karen made an episode out of every little thing. Now, she was making a presentation out of opening a plastic container.

"My friend made brownies, if anybody wants one," Karen said, motioning around the room with the pink bowl. Not that any of them could reach for a brownie, considering they were all attached to IV poles. "I can't eat them. Nothing tastes like it's supposed to," Karen added, "not even brownies."

"That'll get better," Pam said, walking into the room after receiving her weekly booster shot. She smiled at the women. She was their go-to authority on just about anything and everything. "I can taste everything now, but I gained fifteen pounds in the last four months, trying to find something I could taste. Now that food tastes good again, I'm trying to diet. Go figure."

Jessie and Marcie grinned up at Pam from their respective recliners.

"Hey, Pam," Jessie said. "It's great to see you." She felt a sense of relief. Pam seemed to have a way of shutting down Karen's negativity.

Pam walked over and gave Jessie a quick hug and then hugged Marcie and continued around the room to give Irene's hand a squeeze. "How's everyone?" Pam asked. "Counting down the weeks?"

Karen jumped in before anyone else could answer, steering the conversation back to herself. "You gained weight? Gosh, I've lost twenty pounds, which is the only good thing about all of this." She slid the lid back onto the container of untouched chocolate. "Everything else is so awful. This is the worst thing in the world to go through."

Jessie realized that Karen was suddenly fighting back tears. She wanted to feel compassion for her. She had concluded that Karen didn't feel anything for anyone other than herself, but maybe she'd been wrong. Jessie questioned if the tears were authentic or just for show. It was irritating. There was Irene in the far corner, hidden beneath a blanket no thicker than a bed sheet, a mask covering her mouth and nose. She had been there when Jessie had started treatments, and she hadn't heard any of the nurses say anything about her being finished any time soon. And there was Marcie, too young to even be in the green room, staring at Karen with eyes the size of saucers, obviously frightened.

Jessie swallowed and thought for a second about just going back to reading, but Karen's statement hung in the air. Pulling on the side flaps to her wig, she tried a laugh. "Oh, gosh. This isn't the worst thing in the world by far," she said, smiling at the women as a group. "We all have a disease that is treatable. Granted, the treatment is pretty awful, but the doctors can do something about our disease. I'd lots rather lose my hair and my taste buds than my eyesight. Or my arms. Or my legs. Or my mind. This," she said, motioning to the IV pole and catheter running into her chest, "I can deal with all of this."

The women all were staring at her, even Karen, who held the pink container in midair. Pam gave Jessie a bright smile, letting her know she agreed.

The uncomfortable silence was broken when a beeping sound startled them all. In the small room, it was hard to tell the source.

A nurse came from around the partition and walked to Irene's chair. "Looks like you're kinked," she said, straightening out the length of tubing and pressing a button on the machine to stop the noise. She patted Irene's thin hand. "About another hour to go."

As if on cue, Pam stood and wished them all a good day. Before she turned to go, she gave Jessie a bright, conspiratorial smile and pushed open the heavy door.

The four women, still anchored to recliners, busied themselves as best they could and returned to reading or napping, each lost in her own thoughts.

Marcie looked down at the page on her e-reader. She had read the same paragraph a half dozen times and even now couldn't have told anyone what she'd read. She'd listened to the exchange between Karen and Jessie and wrestled with the idea that they both could be right.

This was the worst thing she had ever gone through. She had to agree with Karen about that. Granted, she hadn't lived as many years as the other women, and her life had been pretty much gone the way she had intended: college, short career, marriage, family. It had all been wonderfully ordinary. Until now. She wasn't even supposed to have begun scheduling mammograms yet, but here she was. Originally, her doctor hadn't thought the small lump in her right breast was anything, and neither had Marcie. She wouldn't have even made an appointment to have it checked out if it hadn't been for Emily and Lisa. She was still surprised that she'd followed up on it at all. And in the back of her mind, she hoped she hadn't waited too long.

Shaking off those thoughts, she thought ahead to the rest of the week. Ellie, her seven-year-old daughter, had a soccer game at eight o'clock on Saturday morning and still needed shin guards. A friend had offered the use of her own daughter's used guards, but apparently having your own padded leg protectors was a rite of passage for seven-year-old girls. Plus, they had to match the pink in her team shirt.

Marc's mother had offered to come by early to stay with five-year-old Christopher and three-year-old Madi, so that Marcie didn't have to get them out of bed, dressed, fed, and to the game. That was going to be a huge help, but Marcie wasn't about to leave her home to her mother-in-law without having the laundry done and at least making an attempt to vacuum up dog hair.

Her thoughts returned to the earlier conversation. *Maybe Jessie is right*, she thought. *Maybe this isn't the worst thing in the world. But it kind of feels like it is.*

Her circle of friends had been her lifeline to sanity. They had refused to let her opt out of their weekly get-togethers.

"You have to tell us everything that's going on," Emily had urged, with some humor. "That way, we won't be jealous of you anymore."

The group of young wives and mothers had always teased her for her good fortune of being able to stay at home with the kids, while they held down full-time jobs.

"Yeah, well, this supposedly happens to one in eight women, so I'm your token eight. I'm biting the bullet for the rest of you," Marcie had answered, only partially joking. She had always seemed to be lucky in life: Wonderful parents. A fun, normal childhood. A good husband. Healthy, happy children. And good health. Until cancer. That was the kicker.

On top of everything, she was tired of trying to be optimistic. It was exhausting. She worked at trying to accept what was happening, but so far she hadn't gotten to that point. Maybe the tension that was always just below the surface would gradually dissipate, or maybe she needed it to help her get through this.

She understood Karen's statement that this was the worst thing that could happen. It felt that way a lot of the time. But in her head, she also knew that Jessie was right. There were many things in life worse than this, but knowing that didn't make this any easier.

Chapter 22

Unlike Pam, Karen had always wanted white hair. Her mother had had snowy white hair, without a strand of gray in it. And it had been naturally white, without any chemical help, or none that Karen knew of anyway.

She wondered if her own hair would grow back in white, assuming that it would come back at all. That was always a fear for all of the women, she suspected, although they never talked about that possibility.

Maybe she'd bring it up. She never knew what to say and usually said the wrong thing. Even at a party. *And this is no party*, she thought. She hated the way everyone looked at each other so timidly, hating to ask even the most benign questions for fear of the answer. A simple "How are you?" was now a loaded question.

She was glad to have this Thursday morning over and to be home, finally. The mail was still on the kitchen table, where she had dropped it before going for her chemo. It was mostly bills, to which she'd have to give some attention soon, paying what she could. For many, she sent only the minimum amount. The paycheck was considerably leaner since she had cut back her work hours, not feeling like going in after treatments and being utterly exhausted the following two days. Still, if truth be told, she missed seeing her coworkers as much, if not more, than she missed the bigger paycheck.

She sensed that the other women at the center viewed her as a whiner, but she couldn't help it. They could be as optimistic as they wanted to be, and sure, there were always people in worse circumstances. But this was her life, and from her perspective, it wasn't much of one right now.

The one thing she had going for her was her job. She loved being a part of a group of people, commiserating together in the break room about their schedules, about dealing with grouchy customers—all of it. It gave her a life, especially since Jon had been forced to take disability leave because of his back. Now that he was home all the time, work was her refuge.

Karen pulled out a white plastic sack from the bottom of the stack of mail. The return address showed it was from the wig store she had found online. She turned it over in her hands, hesitant to open it.

She had spent hours browsing the pages and pages of wigs—all colors, styles, and lengths, and all modeled, of course, by healthy, vibrant women. She had finally decided on the pageboy style, in white. Why not? This was her chance to have white hair like her mom. It would be something different, not her usual limp brown hair. She would stand out in a crowd now and not because she was bald. When she'd put eye makeup remover on her head (one of the women—Pam, she thought—had said that would help the hair to grow back in quicker), she had been encouraged to see a faint shadow of growth on her scalp, but it was a light brown color. Of course, she wouldn't be one of those women whose hair came back different and better. Hers would likely come back exactly the same.

Karen had been popular and outgoing as a teenager. Tiny and bubbly, she was the girl all the others wanted as a best friend. She'd been president of the junior class, a majorette with the band, and a cheerleader. She'd had it all going for her, if not in brains or ambition then at least in popularity. Then, she'd gotten pregnant by Jon the summer after her junior year. They had quickly married, and Karen had finished high school via a correspondence course. Those were the days when administrators and school boards thought pregnancy was contagious and that it was best to keep a pregnant girl away from others.

So as Karen was learning to be a wife and terrified by the prospect of giving birth, her girlfriends had continued to cheer on the football team as if a school rivalry and the right game posters were the most important things in the world. Well, that and their hair.

She remembered phoning her best friend, Allie, when the contractions started.

"Oh, how exciting," Allie had said, gushing as if the unbearable pain pushing on Karen's lower back was news she couldn't wait to tell the other girls.

"It really hurts," Karen had cried. "I don't know what to do, Allie. I'm scared. Jon is on his way home, but what if he doesn't get here in time?"

Allie had hesitated, as if her attention was being pulled elsewhere. "Women have babies every day. It can't be that bad."

Karen knew in that instant that she was as far removed from her high school friends as one could possibly get. She was scared and in more pain that she had ever imagined, and she could tell from Allie's tone that she just wanted to get off the phone.

Jon had made it home in time to rush her to the hospital, but their son had been stillborn at two in the morning on a Friday. Their high school friends had stopped by the hospital that evening to offer quick condolences. They were on their way to the football game.

Other than Jon, no one ever mentioned the baby in Karen's presence again. Maybe it seemed to others as if it had never even happened, but Karen's child was never far from her thoughts. Remembering her own comment earlier in the green room, she was ashamed. There were definitely things in life worse than cancer. She knew that better than most.

Karen still stayed in touch with a few of her classmates via Facebook, but she had pretty much stopped sharing any news of herself with the diagnosis of breast cancer. Who wanted to hear about that? Instead, she read the messages from her friends about the cruises they had taken, the activities of their over-achieving children, and their favorite websites for shopping online.

She and Jon had a good marriage, but at some point she had started thinking about their relationship in past tense. They were more friends now than lovers; that was all. Karen was sure that happened to everyone who had been with the same mate for more than thirty years. And that was if they were very lucky.

Maybe the wig would spice up her life, their life. Karen poured herself a glass of iced tea and then sat down at the kitchen table to open the sack, feeling both excitement and trepidation. Well, if it didn't look okay, she'd just send it back. The company had a great return policy: 100 percent satisfaction guaranteed, or just return it for a different style. Nothing ventured, nothing gained. *Of course, nothing ventured, nothing lost either*, Karen thought. She was *trying* to be less pessimistic.

For the past two weeks, she had been wearing a knit cap on her head. It wasn't particularly flattering. The catalog from the online company offered a wide assortment of head-covering options: ball caps with bangs and even ponytails, straw hats with synthetic hair attached to the rim, knit caps in a wide variety of styles and colors, and wigs. Lots of wigs. Karen thought the white pageboy looked classy—such a drastic change from her drab brown hair. And certainly better than the cap.

The wig, folded in half in a clear plastic bag, now looked small and unappealing. A little like a dead white rat. A small card gave directions for its care, along with instructions for how to fit it to one's head, although Karen wasn't sure how anyone could mistake the front of the wig for the back. Still, she thought it was helpful to know that the flaps on the sides were to fit in front of the ears.

She pulled out the piece of synthetic fibers attached to a small patch of netting and gave it all a good shake to loosen the strands.

"Here goes nothing," she said aloud, walking from the kitchen to the bathroom.

Just wait until the girls in the green room see me, she thought and then realized she was smiling for the first time in weeks.

Chapter 23

The first thing Pam noticed when she walked into the green room for her weekly shot the following week was Irene's empty recliner. The second thing was Marcie's ball cap. *Damn, on both accounts*, she thought.

She'd had a pleasant morning, drinking coffee on the back deck and watching the horse in the field behind her home. The mare's only concern, apparently, was food; it was also true, evidently, that the grass truly is greener on the other side of the fence.

The horse belonged to a neighbor, but Pam often took it treats of apple slices or carrots. The animal behaved as if Pam were a long-lost friend, often nuzzling her palm and reaching over the fence after eating the treat to make sure that the bowl she carried was really empty. She'd thought about asking the neighbor if she could ride with her sometime, but she hadn't followed up on it. Probably wasn't a good idea now. Bouncing was not in her treatment plan, and just the thought of it was frightening. *One more thing off the bucket list*, she thought, *just not crossed off as having been done*.

From the deck, she could pretend the house was in the country. The back area of the property was a field, bordered by trees, brush, and wildflowers. The front view was of more homes similar to hers, some nearly identical, in fact, with only different front doors and landscaping to set them apart. Pam didn't mind. They had bought the house for its view from the back anyway.

Stephen would have loved this morning, with the crisp air and peaceful view of the grazing horse. He *had* loved it. After two years, it still didn't seem possible that he was gone.

While they'd been dealing with her numerous doctor appointments, tests, outcomes, and treatment options, he had been diagnosed with prostate cancer and had died before Pam had even finished her year-long treatment plan.

She knew it wasn't rational, but she blamed herself for his death. Emotions, stress, lack of sleep—everything she'd read on the Internet confirmed that these factors contributed to poor health and the possibility of disease. Add to that the fact that she'd been so focused on herself that she hadn't noticed that Stephen wasn't himself, wasn't feeling well, and that it had nothing to do with his worrying over her. By the time they both realized he was ill, it was too late.

Cancer didn't wait for you to be able to handle it.

She hadn't told the women in the green room about her situation. Surely they had to notice that she never talked about a husband, but they probably thought she was divorced, and Pam let them think it. It wasn't as if she didn't want to talk about her husband, about how wonderful a man he had been, about how much she missed him or even how responsible she felt for his death. She just couldn't share all of that with them. Yet. She told herself that she didn't want to add to the stress that her green-room friends were feeling by sharing her personal sorrow. But the truth was she just didn't want to add to her own by having it out there. It would be another reason for people to look at her with pity and sadness, and she'd had enough of that.

"Everyone is just concerned about you," a friend had told her.

Well, concern looks an awful lot like pity, Pam thought. Plus, she appreciated the attitude of the other women in the chemo room toward her. She was a few years older than Jessie and Karen and considerably older than Marcie. She was finished with chemo and well on her way to being done with radiation too. The others looked to her as something of a torch-bearer, for information on what to expect in their own treatments and with assurance that everything could and would be okay.

This morning, with the absence of Irene and the addition of Marcie's ball cap, Pam hoped that would be true for all of them.

"Hospital. Blood count was down," Jessie said, catching Pam's glance toward the corner where Irene usually sat.

Pam shook her head. "She's had a tough go of it. She seemed okay last Thursday."

"This is the first week since I started that she's been gone," Jessie said. "Of course, the nurses won't tell us anything."

Pam smiled, glancing away from the empty recliner. "Yeah, I know. But that's a good thing, I guess. No news is good news. I hope Irene stays on the Thursday schedule."

Jessie smiled, understanding Pam's statement. While Irene rarely, if ever, joined conversations in the green room, she was a steady presence. The sight of her in her cap and mask, sitting in the same chair every week, shouldn't have been comforting. But it was.

Pam smiled at Marcie, who looked even younger in skinny jeans and now a Saint Louis Cardinals ball cap. "You look about fourteen," Pam said. "I'm all ears in a cap. You look darling."

Marcie wiggled her head, a smile breaking across her pale face. "You think?"

"Absolutely! You rock that look."

Marcie laughed, pulling on the brim of the cap. "Ah, so now that we've established how young I look, we're going to throw down some slang? Well, girlfriend, I think *you* rock that look."

Pam exaggerated the movement of tweaking her spiky blonde hair, pulling the tips straight up. "We're just BFFs with new looks," she said with a laugh.

"Yeah, I guess," Marcie said, her laugh fading. "You warned me. Eighteen days. Thought I might get lucky and keep it."

Karen opened a bag of lemon drops, took one, and passed it on. "Thank God for wigs," she said. She had started wearing her white pageboy, and although she worried that it made her look older, she was enjoying it. "Sure doesn't take long to get ready to go anywhere these days. Not that I go many places."

Although Pam was free to leave, having been there only for blood work, she took an empty chair and sat down with her friends. She smiled at Karen. "Still going into work?"

Karen nodded. "I love my job. And the people there. I can't quit, or I'd miss out on the latest gossip."

The others laughed with her.

"Feeling okay?" Pam took a lemon drop from the bag.

"Still losing weight," Karen answered. "I feel okay, I think. Sometimes I wonder if I remember what feeling good feels like, you know? Food still tastes weird, although we did go out for Mexican food the other night, and it was wonderful. *That* I could taste. That, and these lemon drops. Plus, my doctor says these will help keep my mouth moist. I guess it's important for our gums. I didn't realize chemo could cause dental problems. One more thing, I guess."

"What kind of dental problems?" Marcie reached out her hand for a drop.

"Dry mouth. Receding gums. Tooth decay. Plus sore throats. One fun thing after another," Karen answered.

Pam, certain that Karen was headed straight for her rant about how all of this was the end of the world and the worst thing that could ever happen, tried a diversionary tactic. "Where did you eat?" she asked. "I love Mexican food."

"We just went to the place in the mall; can't remember the name of it," Karen answered. "It's a chain, I think. But we knew it would be quicker than anywhere downtown, and we were going to a movie afterward."

Jessie was quiet, remembering the devastating experience she'd had in the same restaurant a few weeks ago.

"I can't remember the last time I went to a movie," Pam said, realizing it had to have been before Stephen died. *Another life marker*, she thought. "What did you see? Lots of good shows out right now."

"Well, we couldn't agree," Karen said, "So I gave in, and we saw the 3-D action movie that Jon wanted to see. Might not have been the best idea. Felt like I might throw up throughout the whole show, you know, the way things come right at you? But the popcorn was good. And Jon liked it. He gets turned on by all that violence."

The other women laughed with her.

"Maybe I should get Marc to take me to see it," Marcie said. "It would be great if *something* turned him on." She had tried to sound lighthearted and funny, but her words came out sounding sad and pathetic, even to her.

Marcie had met Marc through a mutual friend while both were still in college. Conversation had been easy from the very beginning, and they had a chemistry that had moved the relationship into a serious one faster than either had expected. As twenty-two-year-olds, they had thought they were destined to be together. Now she wondered.

She had read enough on the Internet to know that marital problems were on the list of cancer's hidden side effects. The vows might include "in sickness and in health," but that's on the wedding day, pledged while wearing a fairy-tale dress and standing in front of family and friends. No one really believes sickness will be an issue. And no one signs up for cancer.

So far, though, Marc had been okay about everything she was going through, at least when he was in town. The company he worked for had arranged for him to take jobs close to home, so that was a help, especially with the kids. Marc had even offered to sit with her in the green room, but it seemed half-hearted, and Marcie hadn't encouraged him.

"Why would you want to sit for three hours? I'm going to be reading anyway. Go to work. You'll be happier, and so will I," she told him. "Seriously, Marc. I don't want you there. I'll be worried that you're bored, and I'll feel like I have to entertain you. Believe me; there's nothing entertaining in a chemotherapy room."

In fact, Marcie thought, Karen's husband was the only one to have visited, and she had seemed almost relieved when he left. Karen hadn't told the women that Jon used a walker due to his back injury and that it made him seem so much older than he was. Marcie recalled how Karen introduced him to the others and made them sound like closer friends than they were. At least, Marcie thought, Karen made an effort to complain less while Jon was there.

Marcie knew Marc would be miserable, trying to figure out what to say to these other women. Still, she wished he'd ask her more about how she felt and what the treatment entailed. He acted as if he was afraid to even touch her. She'd experienced acquaintances keeping a good distance during conversations with her, as if they might breathe the same air and catch the same disease. But that wasn't it with Marc.

She suspected that he truly was appalled that she'd had part of a breast removed. She hadn't allowed him to be in the room during examinations following surgery, and now she wished she hadn't been afraid of that. Yes, her breast was indented and there were scars, but it wasn't so horrific. Was it?

She missed his touch. Not just the sex, though she certainly did miss that, but the intimacy of a passionate kiss, of an embrace that wasn't cautious. She wanted him to back her up against a wall and kiss her the way he used to. Granted, he hadn't done that for years, but she could remember the thrill. She hadn't realized, when this all started, that it might be the end of their sex life.

She wished she could ask Pam about that. Maybe down the road, she would. She didn't know Pam's circumstances; she had never mentioned a man in her life, but surely there was one. Or more. Marcie knew Pam had stepchildren; she had talked about both Adam and Anne, and it seemed like they had a good relationship. Pam was such an attractive woman and more so now that her hair was coming back. She could pull off a pixie cut like a movie star.

Marcie wasn't sure what she would do about her own hair—or rather, the absence of it. Continuing to wearing a ball cap hardly seemed like an ideal solution, but she had looked over some of the wigs in the private exam rooms and didn't like the looks of any of them. They were available to "borrow," but she couldn't help thinking each one might have been on hundreds of other heads before hers. And while she didn't like thinking it, she also wondered how many of those other women had died.

She'd looked online for wigs, but it seemed such an act of desperation to buy hair. Two wig catalogs were hidden under a notebook on her desk at home. Both companies offered not only wigs but special bras and fake breasts. *Now, that would really turn Marc on*, she thought.

At home after the treatment, Marcie grabbed a bottle of water from the fridge and carried it out onto the back patio, which was a ten-foot-by-ten-foot slab of concrete. She had clipped magazine photos of what she envisioned it becoming someday: stonework around the pool, permanent seating, a fire pit—but it was all on hold for now, like everything else in their lives. It seemed like the only things moving forward were her treatments, doctor appointments, blood work, and so on. Marcie hated how the cancer had taken control of their lives. There were now too many unknowns, and she was hesitant to plan very far ahead.

Before all of this, she had enjoyed change and making things happen. The youngest of four, she knew she'd been spoiled and had been given more advantages than her siblings. It wasn't necessarily her parents' design. Life had just been simpler for them by the time she came along. Money wasn't as tight then; plus, they'd known she was definitely their last child and had treated her as such.

Honestly, Marcie couldn't remember a time that she wasn't happy. She'd loved growing up on a farm and had spent most of her childhood outdoors. She especially loved horses, a passion she shared with Pam. Her dad had put out barrels in the pasture, and Marcie had spent many sunny days racing her horse around them, thrilled with the speed as much as the sense of competition, even if it was only against herself.

She'd had friends during her high school years, but she preferred her time at home, caring for her growing collection of pets that included an orphaned fawn, numerous cats, and always more than one dog.

The day before she was to leave for college, she'd gone for a ride through the pasture to a watershed pond. She'd loosely tied the horse's reins to a tall sapling and sat down on the scrub grass, thinking of what lay ahead. She hadn't realized her dad had driven his truck to the other side of the pond until he slid down on the ground to sit beside her.

"You okay?" he had asked quietly, putting his arm around her shoulders. "You're not scared to go off to college, are you?"

She remembered telling him that no, she wasn't afraid. But she was something. Nervous? Apprehensive? Unprepared? "I just wonder what my life will be," she had finally answered.

He had hugged her harder and laughed. "I imagine it will be whatever you want it to be."

Marcie had believed him. She'd graduated from college with a degree in marketing, had worked at a job she loved, and had married a wonderful man who had given her three beautiful and loving children.

Now she had cancer, and the ground felt shaky beneath her feet. She wanted back the confidence that she had enjoyed in her youth.

She sat down in one of the plastic Adirondack chairs they were using until she could decide on what she really wanted and glanced down at her flower beds. She had planted bulbs right after they'd moved in, although she couldn't remember what kind. Daffodils, for sure. Tulips, maybe. It seemed like some other flower too, but she couldn't recall. She'd planted them so late in the season after their move to the new house that she'd be surprised if they came up at all. The beds were covered with leaves. She thought, momentarily, of going to the garage for a rake, but just the thought exhausted her. The bulbs would either push their way up or not. She allowed herself a brief moment of self-pity, wondering if she'd even be around to see the flowers bloom.

Why was she being so morbid? Of course she'd be here through spring, into summer, and finally fall. By then, this would all be behind her.

By fall, all of this would be over. Fall had always been her favorite season. While in college, she and Marc rarely missed a football game, donning team jerseys to join the crowd tailgating in the parking lot. Marcie had loved everything about it: the camaraderie, the smells, the tastes, the laughter, the slight chill in the air that had them all wearing sweatshirts until halftime and then stripping them off to celebrate in T-shirts. Her long dark hair was typically pulled into a ponytail that bobbed in the sunshine through the back of her ball cap.

It made her smile even now to think of those lazy Saturday afternoons filled with friends and noise. They didn't live far from a university town but had gone to only one game in the last ten years. It just wasn't the same, sitting in the grown-up section and watching the college kids' antics. Although only in their thirties, she and Marc had felt ancient by comparison. Had they really had that much energy and been that carefree once upon a time? Plus, such an outing now meant either hiring a sitter or taking three restless kids along, which they had done the last time they'd seen a game. Neither she nor Marc had particularly enjoyed the afternoon. She envied young mothers who lived close enough to their parents to have help with child care—and free care at that.

Still, on game days both she and Marc would usually wear college sweatshirts and fix snack foods to enjoy while watching the televised game at home. If she had to admit it, these days were more fun than the ordeal of attending a game in person. She could kick off her shoes, nestle into her overstuffed chair, cover herself with an afghan, and enjoy the game in comfort.

Unless it was a close contest (or if the kids were demanding to be entertained), she usually napped during at least part of the game. Napping had become a new favorite pastime, more so now that her energy level was at an all-time low.

Picking up her water bottle, she headed back indoors. The kids were at school for a few more hours, and Marc was out of town—again. Sleepy from the warmth of the sun, she was glad there was time for a decent nap.

Plus, it would be heaven to have her bare head (she refused to use the word "bald") uncovered for a few hours. Like Marc, the kids had never seen her without a cap since she had lost her hair. She set the alarm on her cell phone, guaranteeing that she'd be up and fully covered before they got home from school.

It seemed as though she had just put her head on the pillow when she felt the comforter being tugged and heard Christopher's small voice.

"Mom?"

Marcie jumped as if she'd been shot, sitting upright and staring into her son's frightened eyes. It took a moment before she realized what had scared him.

"Mommy?"

"Go, Chris!" She saw tears welling in his eyes and realized how harshly the words had come out. Softening her voice, she added, "I'll be up in a minute, sweetie."

Christopher backed slowly away and then turned and ran. Marcie could hear him racing upstairs to his bedroom.

Oh, God, she thought. She hadn't wanted her children to see her without hair. It was bad enough when she looked in the mirror herself and saw a reflection of a woman she barely recognized. In addition to being bald, her scalp was red, bruised, and slightly swollen. The lack of hair only made her eyes look more dull and sunken.

After splashing her face with cold water and putting on a little blush and mascara, she pulled on her wig and made her way to Christopher's room, knocking lightly and then pushing open the door.

Her son was face down on his bed, his little shoulders shaking. Marcie scooted him over and sat down beside him, placing her hand on his small back.

"Chris," she whispered. "I'm sorry I sounded so cranky. You just surprised me."

He rolled over to his back and looked up at her, his eyes huge. "Are you going to die?" he asked.

Marcie gathered him up in her arms, burying her face in his soft hair, fighting tears of her own. She held him that way and then pushed back to look into his eyes. "I'm not going to die, Chris. Not for a long, long, long time. Not until I am really, really old. I promise. Okay?"

His look was challenging. "What happened to your hair?"

Marcie smiled. She was continually amazed at the quick change of a child's mind. Choosing her words carefully, she explained, as simply as possible, that she had been sick, and the doctors were giving her medicine that would make her well. "But the medicine made my hair fall out," she said, holding his gaze and forcing a smile.

Christopher stared back at her, his eyes showing he was trying to understand all of this, to make some kind of sense from what she was telling him. "That's weird," he said, shaking his head. "Medicine never makes my hair fall out."

Marcie tousled his hair, hopeful that the hardest part of the conversation was over. "I know, and that's a good thing. You have pretty cool hair. My medicine is just really strong, but I won't have to take it much longer," she said.

"And then your hair will come back?" Christopher asked.

"That's right," Marcie answered, "but until it does, I'll wear this wig. I'm sorry you saw me without it on. I didn't want you to."

"That's okay, Mom," her son answered, sounding suddenly very grown up for his five years. "I won't tell anybody."

Chapter 24

Pam stood at the open closet door. It was time, she knew, but could she do it? Suit jackets, pressed white shirts, a full belt hanger, a shoe rack full of designer styles—someone should get some use from Stephen's clothing. She had read in the newspaper about a nonprofit program to help the unemployed "dress for success," and it was just enough motivation to get her started. Stephen had always laughed at her opinion that clothes made the man, particularly for a job. She still believed it. One of these suits could change another man's life forever; perhaps give him a leg up in the job market. They weren't doing anyone any good, including Pam, hanging in their walk-in closet, where she saw them every day as she picked out her own clothes.

Not that choosing clothes had been much of a task for months, as she had pretty much lived in jeans and fleece zip-up tops after her surgery and while going through chemo and radiation. Easy in, easy out. And soft on tender skin. Soon, she would be going back to work as a manager for a nationwide industry that made high-end cabinet products. She loved her job and was thankful that they had held her position open for her—thankful but not surprised. She was very good at managing the multitude of details and tasks that came up on a daily basis and wondered now what had been happening since her last visit, when she stopped to see if there were any issues she could help with. She had ended up staying most of the day, coming home more exhausted than she should have been.

She only hoped she was as valuable to the company as it was to her. Since her diagnosis and Stephen's soon after, their simultaneous illnesses; the multitude of tests, appointments, and treatments; and Stephen's final weeks at a hospice center and then his death, the job was her lifeline to some degree of sanity.

The bed was soon covered with dress clothing ready to donate. Even so, Stephen's side of the closet was still full of clothes, but these would be harder to discard—casual shirts and jackets, sweatshirts, team jerseys, and a stack of blue jeans. While Pam had enjoyed seeing Stephen dressed in a classy suit, she'd loved him the most when he'd pull on a pair of jeans and a favorite threadbare T-shirt. Dressed up, Stephen was handsome; dressed down, he was sexy as hell. God, she missed him.

They had met at Pam's office. Stephen, a lawyer, had come for a meeting with management to review their standard contract with buyers. Pam had been asked to sit in, as any changes made to the procedure would be her job to enforce. There had been a spark between them from the first handshake. Stephen was four years older and had seemed to Pam to be the epitome of an upwardly mobile professional man. He had teased her later that she'd been a breath of fresh air in the stale climate of contract law. Divorced for two years, he'd been dating for a while but wasn't looking for a wife, he'd said, until he met Pam. Likewise, she was enjoying her career and definitely not looking for a husband.

They were married four months later. The courtship had been fun and tender; the early months of marriage were as happy as they were hectic. Stephen and Pam enjoyed having his kids for scattered weekends and school vacations and had even taken them on a fishing trip once, which had turned out to be a disaster when Adam and Anne realized there was no Internet service in a campground.

The kids had enjoyed the home Stephen bought after marrying Pam, and they had spent countless lazy afternoons around the pool.

Their teen years were fun for both Stephen and Pam, with the house always full and noisy, packed with energetic boys and girls.

When Pam was diagnosed with breast cancer, they had shielded the kids from the news, only telling them what was necessary as the disease and treatment impacted her appearance and energy.

A few months later, when Stephen received his heartbreaking diagnosis, they had sat Adam and Anne down and told them what was happening with both their dad and their stepmom, and Pam saw the same anger in them that she felt herself. It was all so unfair.

It had seemed to Pam that the kids' anger at the whole situation landed on her, as if their dad wouldn't be dying if he had never married her. A friend suggested counseling, if not for the whole family then at least for Pam, to help her see life clearly and to learn to cope.

Oh, I see life pretty clearly. Thank you very much, Pam had thought, though she told her friend that she'd consider it.

But there wasn't much to think about. Or maybe there was too much. Most days she couldn't have said which was the case. Maybe Stephen's kids were right. Maybe everything that had happened was because of her. She'd tried to recall the specifics of a story about a pebble falling down a mountain, causing a disaster a continent away. Maybe she, in some way, was the cause of his illness.

And maybe the kids didn't think she was to blame at all. Maybe she just thought they did.

Pam shook her head, trying to dispel the gloomy thoughts. Going forward was hard enough without giving way to the backward pull. Her husband had died, taking with him her hopes and dreams. Now, it was time for a new plan. Management was her thing, after all.

The backseat of her SUV was now heaped with Stephen's clothes. *The leisure clothes can wait for another day*, she thought. This was an already huge move in a new direction.

With her arms laden with the rich fabrics, she determinedly carried them into the offices of the nonprofit agency. The girl at the front desk barely looked up from the magazine she'd been reading when Pam pushed open the door with her shoulder, but she led the way to a table in a back room, where an already enormous amount of garments were waiting to be sorted.

The girl looked at Pam questioningly. "Oh, my," she said. "Are you sure about donating these? They're so nice. Beautiful. Nicer than anything I've seen come in. Well, nicer than anything I've seen. Period."

"I'm sure," Pam said, refusing to look down at the stack of Stephen's clothes. She walked with a sense of purpose back out the door.

Only when she was again in the car did she allow herself to relax, and the feeling surprised her. She had expected to feel sorrow but instead felt amazingly lighter, happier even. She sincerely hoped the clothes would be put to good use and appreciated by whoever received them, but really, it wasn't her issue to manage any more. It felt good.

Also, the closet was emptier, and that was a good thing. It was a start toward emptying out the rest of their home. Even with a decent paycheck from her own job and Stephen's life insurance, she doubted she'd be able to keep the house. At least, she was pretty sure she wouldn't. She'd planned to call their accountant for months but continued to put it off. Knowing her financial situation was one thing; having someone she respected state the facts aloud was another altogether. Their financial picture had seemed so bright only months ago. The constant drain on the budget from expenses not covered by insurance was another side effect of cancer.

She wasn't ready to accept that she could no longer afford this house. Maybe she didn't want to keep it anyway. It was too big for one person. She hadn't thought that all out yet. One thing at a time. She had loved their home, but without Stephen, it was just a house. She hoped that she'd be able to convince herself of that and move on.

Although finished with surgery, chemo, and radiation, Pam still felt the aftershocks in fatigue, lethargy, and a constant battle against depression. The idea that she might be helping others—through the donation of clothes and in trying to be an example for the other women in the green room—gave her a sense of purpose until she could return to work full time.

She looked forward to that. She wanted to wear her nice clothes again, to have stimulating conversations, to be respected for her mind, and to come home at the end of the day with mental fatigue, not physical exhaustion.

Plus, it would be great to have a steady paycheck automatically deposited into her bank account. When the company had granted her a leave of absence with the promise of holding her position open, she'd been relieved and delighted. But she missed the paychecks from working full time. She'd been going in for a few hours a week and had told her boss that she would be ready to come back full time at the beginning of the coming month.

And then what? The idea of being single again, with her job the largest part of her life, was depressing. She had lived that existence. Stephen had shown her how full life could be. She wanted that life again, but she suspected she would forever hold other men up to Stephen and find them lacking.

Chapter 25

Karen had been excited about losing weight, especially since she had put no effort into it. But three weeks of shedding pounds had left her looking older than her age, and her limbs felt weak and useless.

She had read that most women gained weight during chemo, especially those who were also on steroids to help manage nausea and to trick the body into not fighting the chemicals fed into the veins to kill cells. She had been telling herself that she was one of the lucky ones, but she knew otherwise. She looked gaunt and old. The white wig probably didn't help, but still, she liked it.

It had been years, decades even, since she'd been to a gym. She and a group of friends had taken aerobic classes in their twenties. They often went for drinks and snacks afterward, which defeated the purpose of exercise, but it was a fun night out. But working out at a gym would be a different story. She hadn't told anyone she was going to start, other than the oncologist. He had encouraged her, saying it was a great idea for building stamina in addition to improving her mood. Dr. Park did caution her against using weights, and she had chuckled. Yeah, she'd told him, like she planned on doing that.

But the idea did take some planning. She bought brightly colored sneakers and a pair of yoga pants, and those two purchases alone did wonders for her mood. Karen thought about calling Jessie so that she wouldn't have to walk into the gym alone but quickly dropped that idea. They had all exchanged phone numbers, but none of them had used them. At least, Karen didn't think they had. Maybe the others got together and hadn't included her, but she didn't think so. With all of the complaining she'd done in the green room, it would have been understandable. Even she realized she was a drag to be around. The other women going through treatment had made her aware of that, simply by their positive attitudes, and she was working to be a more enjoyable person.

Wearing her new workout clothes, she drove to the fitness center, which was attached to a wing of the hospital. Taking a deep breath, she summoned up the nerve to enter.

After paying the membership fee and getting a twenty-minute tour of the place by a twentysomething "coach," she spent the next twenty-five minutes on the bike. She pumped her legs until she wasn't sure they'd hold her up when she decided to quit, but they had. And the doctor was right; her mood, while not exactly optimistic, was greatly improved.

She hadn't worked hard enough to break a sweat, so she left on her exercise clothes. When she got home, Jon noticed, and that was another plus.

"Well, look at you," he said. He dropped his jacket onto the back of a chair and came around the kitchen counter to give her a quick kiss. "You look cute. Have you been out walking?"

"Nope. I actually went to the gym and rode a bicycle for about half an hour," Karen answered.

Jon smiled a different smile than the tense everything-is-going-to-be-okay smile he usually gave her. "Well, good for you. That's great," he said. "What prompted that?"

His arms were still around her waist, and Karen leaned back into him. It felt so good to have him really embracing her and not acting as if she might break in half.

"I don't know, really," she said. "I just feel like I need to do something to get stronger. And it really did feel great. I'm going to try to go on a regular schedule. Every other day, maybe. Other than chemo days, that is."

"And it's okay to work out?"

"Yeah. Dr. Park said it would be great for me, as long as I don't do any lifting."

She could feel Jon's grin even before she turned to see it. "Ah, still no running the vacuum cleaner?"

It had become a joke between them since one of her early visits to the oncologist. As usual, Jon had gone with her. The specialist had explained what she could and couldn't do after a lumpectomy.

In his usual style that had made Karen fall in love with him, Jon had jokingly asked if she'd be able to clean house. Dr. Park had laughed.

"Well, think you feel up to that?" he had asked Karen.

She had played along, pretending to give it serious thought. "Hmm. I think it might be a little too soon. Maybe in a year or so. We'll see."

All three had laughed, and the mood in the exam room had lifted.

It was Jon's sense of humor that had seen them through so much in life. It had certainly helped when he'd been hurt at work—a back injury that the doctors cautioned could turn into a permanent disability. The jury was still out on that. Jon and Karen had thought that would the biggest challenge they'd face, next to losing their son so many years ago. Nothing compared to that loss. And it hadn't been easy dealing with the changes that came from Jon's being at home and Karen's becoming the breadwinner. His doctors were optimistic that he'd regain some of his strength, and surgery was a consideration, but that was on hold, both because Karen's health had become the first priority and because of finances.

While money had always been tight, it was the realization that they would never have children that had been the true challenge to their marriage. After trying for years and going through individual fertility tests, they had borrowed money for an in vitro treatment. Karen had miscarried at three months. The doctor predicted that with all of the hormones in her system, she'd likely be pregnant again within a few months, and she was. Again, she miscarried in the third month.

It was enough. They had tried, and neither felt emotionally strong enough to try again. Now, both in their early fifties, pregnancy wasn't an option. Jon had suggested looking into adoption or perhaps fostering a child or children, but Karen didn't have the emotional energy to consider either possibility. Now, with her fighting breast cancer and Jon still dealing with his back pain, plus their ages, they wouldn't likely be successful candidates for either option. Nieces and nephews on both sides of the family would have to be enough to fill the longing for children to love and nurture. Karen had accepted that it would be just the two of them. She didn't know if Jon had.

Losing a child when they were still children themselves and then the stress of trying to get pregnant again for so many years had made lovemaking more of a chore than a pleasure for more years than Karen could remember.

Maybe Jon would want to talk about becoming foster parents again, once all of this was behind them, but honestly, Karen hoped not. The years were going by, and the clang of the biological clock that was so loud in her thirties and even into her early forties had grown quiet. If their baby had lived, he or she would be an adult now and maybe a parent as well.

She thought about the other women from the green room. Pam talked about her grown stepchildren occasionally. It sounded like she had a good relationship with them. She knew Jessie had grown children. She had shared how hard it had been to tell them about her cancer. Irene rarely talked at all, keeping herself hidden behind the gauze mask, so Karen didn't know if she was a mother or not; if so, she was likely a grandmother as well.

Marcie talked often about her three children, sometimes to the point that Karen felt like screaming. She didn't know how the younger woman managed to care for a husband, three small kids, and her home; stay involved with friends;

and still go through what she was going through. *The only answer*, Karen thought, *is that Marcie is young.*

Karen had accepted that her life would center on Jon, and that was okay. More than okay, in fact. He was not only her husband; he was her best friend. If she was truthful, he had been her only friend until she started working.

And she loved her job. Oh, she knew what people said, what they thought. *Is that as high as your aspirations go? Working at a discount store?* But she truly did love it, and she was good at it. She'd started in housewares but had quickly proved her work ethic, intelligence, and dedication and had been promoted to manager of the paint department. She enjoyed studying the new sheets of colors that could be developed and making sure the display of samples was always full and the paint displays organized. She liked going to management meetings, giving reports, and scheduling the employees. It was what she imagined owning her own small business might be like—the satisfaction of a job well done, only without the financial fears of being on your own.

Mostly she enjoyed her coworkers, who shared their life stories over coffee breaks, celebrated good news together, and had each other's backs during tough times. Like now. During the first few weeks of chemo, she hadn't cooked a single meal. Her coworkers had filled their freezer with casseroles, soups, and lasagna and had occasionally dropped off complete meals, including desserts. They knew her love of chocolate, which was apparent in the brownies, cookies, and pies they had delivered.

What they hadn't known was that she couldn't taste any of it. If they'd noticed that she had lost weight—so much that it was short of attractive—no one mentioned it.

The exercise would help, she thought now, both with her flabby muscles and with improving her attitude. While the women in the green room put up with her moods, when she had started grumbling to coworkers about how awful it was to go through all of this, she'd caught a few of them avoiding her when she'd walk through the aisles on her way to the break room. She didn't blame them. She didn't like being around herself these days.

It was time for that to change.

Chapter 26

The chemotherapy room was quiet. It was a relatively small area, especially compared to the centers built for that purpose alone at the larger metropolitan hospital, where Dr. Nathan Park was also on staff. Each week, he visited three of these makeshift centers, created so patients going through chemo wouldn't have to drive hours from their homes. It wasn't an ideal plan, but it was better than only a few years ago, when cancer patients died simply because lifesaving care wasn't available nearby.

This center's three-person staff had tried to make it comfortable, but it certainly wasn't cheerful. Potted plants struggled on the window sills, while one smaller plant fought for space on a crowded cart holding a coffeepot and packets of sweeteners and creamers. A tube of Styrofoam cups lay nearby. The coffee was brewed every morning, but Dr. Park had yet to see a patient fix a cup. Maybe they did on treatment days, when they'd be staying for several hours, but the days when they met with him were short by comparison. He knew they just wanted to get in and get out. He couldn't blame them.

Although he'd driven ninety miles to be here by seven in the morning, it was worth it. Dr. Park appreciated the early morning solitude before other staff came in at eight, and patients began arriving soon after that. He let himself in through the back door, near which a small sign reading Cancer Center had been attached, and made his way through the semidarkness to the office. The staff would have made everything ready for him the previous afternoon; charts, lab reports, and notes on any of their concerns about patients would be stacked in a neat pile in an area they had set up for him.

He sipped the to-go coffee he'd picked up at the convenience store down the street and put a hand on the stack of patient files. He'd likely see twenty to twenty-five patients today, all of them undergoing some type of chemotherapy on different days of the week. The schedule was designed for him to have fifteen minutes with each patient. Some exams were shorter, others longer. Some patients wanted more explanation of what was going on than others. Some patients brought family members or friends with them, and those visits took longer, but Dr. Park didn't object. Family and friends were often more involved than the patients themselves, wanting to hear that everything that could be done was being done. He understood. The patients had enough to deal with on a daily basis—the changes in their bodies, managing the side effects of chemo, scheduling appointments for blood work and checkups—and all of that in addition to the tasks and duties they were juggling before cancer pushed its way into their lives.

After medical school and during his residency, he'd thought he wanted to be a family practitioner. The idea of seeing all ages and both genders appealed to him. But as he found himself devoting any extra time he could find to reading the latest studies on cancer and its treatments, he made the difficult decision to add more years to his education to become an oncologist. Cancer and its causes remained largely a medical mystery, but advancements in the field were encouraging. A diagnosis was no longer a death sentence, as it had been fewer than twenty years ago.

And unfortunately, even as an oncologist, he still saw people of all ages.

His nurses constantly teased him that his bedside manner needed work, but he had learned that his patients appreciated his honest, straightforward attitude. Cancer couldn't be sugar-coated. His ever-growing number of patients couldn't afford platitudes, and he wouldn't give them. He told it like it was, the good news and the bad.

And he knew he'd be delivering both today. He had only to study the files to determine which patient would leave the exam room with renewed energy and hope and which would walk away in shock and resignation.

Chapter 27

Marcie grabbed another orange from the kitchen drainer and set about cutting it into quarters on the chopping block. She was glad to be doing something normal, trying to keep her mind off of today's appointment with Dr. Park. It was always scary. She liked the doctor, and she didn't have any real reason to fear that he would give her bad news. But you never knew. She still had trouble accepting that she even had an oncologist. She'd been tolerating the chemo, if you didn't count the loss of hair, eyebrows, and eyelashes; the thin, peeling fingernails; a fuzzy mind she'd learned was called "chemo brain"; and the death of taste buds.

The sweet, tangy smell of the oranges was refreshing. Why didn't she ever cut some up just for her family to have with breakfast or dinner? She answered her own question: because they wouldn't eat them. Getting fruit—or vegetables, for that matter—into their diets was an ongoing challenge.

These oranges were for Ellie's after-school soccer game. She dumped the wedges into a green plastic bowl and fit the lid on tightly so the treats wouldn't spill in the tote bag, which was already packed with bottles of water and sunscreen.

Christopher and Madi were excited for the game. They loved an outing of any kind and were happy to play under the bleachers in the dirt with their friends or to sprawl across the grass at her feet with books and markers. All three kids would come home dirty and tired, but that was okay with Marcie. Early baths and pajamas; then they'd enjoy an evening of watching a movie or playing a board game before bed. A good day all around, she hoped. First, she had to get through her appointment.

Marc was working close to home and had promised to get away in time to pick up Christopher and Madi from preschool. Both were now in school all day, which had been a huge adjustment for Marcie. She had concerns about enrolling their baby in an all-day center, but it had been a good move. Madi loved it, and Marcie was getting used to the quiet. Some days, she missed their trips to the mall or to McDonald's, with the sound of constant chatter and bickering coming from their child seats behind her, but it was also a blessing that they weren't younger. Some days, she just didn't have the energy for them.

Ellie was going home with a teammate after school and would ride with that family to the game. Marcie mentally checked off the details, hoping Ellie hadn't forgotten her shin guards. Doubtful. She loved them, even to the point of wearing them around the house for no apparent reason. Everyone was covered; she'd meet them at the game after her doctor's appointment.

The visit with Dr. Park, however, didn't go as expected. He was concerned about a small bump near the scars from her lumpectomy.

"It's likely scar tissue," he said quietly, putting a hand on her arm, "but I'd like to get a biopsy to make sure."

Marcie felt her blood turn cold. Her voice didn't even sound like her own. "A biopsy? Another biopsy? So what does that mean? What is it you want to be sure of?"

To his credit, Dr. Park continued to look steadily into her eyes. "I'd like to schedule a biopsy so that we know what we're dealing with."

"What does that mean?" Marcie repeated.

Dr. Park remained firm. "Let's get the biopsy done and talk again. We'll know more then."

She fought the panic growing inside her and locked eyes with the oncologist. "Are you saying that I *still* have cancer? That I now have a *different* cancer?"

"Marcie, I'm saying we need information on this new lump," Dr. Park answered. "You told me at our first meeting that you wanted to be aggressive, that you would do whatever you had to do to fight this and live a long, healthy life. Let's do what we have to do to assure that. Okay?"

Marcie felt like she had taken a hard fist to her stomach. She was suddenly cold and could feel the frost deep in her veins. Sitting in the exam room, she stole a quick look at her watch. She couldn't be late for the soccer game. She had promised Ellie. Plus, she was the mom with the orange slices. She didn't have time to deal with this. This was supposed to be a routine monthly meeting with her oncologist. She'd handled the surgery without any problem. She was halfway through chemo. Now, it seemed that having her left breast mutilated and losing her hair, her energy, her appetite, and life as she knew it wasn't enough.

Dr. Park squeezed her arm. "Marcie, let's find out what we're dealing with, not what we can imagine it might be."

Marcie only nodded. She left the office with assurances from the staff that they would contact Dr. Catterson to schedule a biopsy. She hated the look of concern in their eyes and knew if she gave in to the panic she was feeling, she might not come back out of it. It felt like the first day of this nightmare all over again. No, that wasn't true. This was worse. Because she had thought she was on the path to the other side, and apparently, she was back to square one. She couldn't go through everything all over again. She couldn't.

She didn't remember driving to the soccer fields. Her mind was numb, even as she fought the shaking in her limbs. She parked and made her way to the bleachers, through parents and grandparents setting up lawn chairs, pulling her cap on more firmly over her bald head and pasting on a smile. *I should have worn my wig*, she thought. She had finally borrowed one from the center but rarely wore it. She felt hidden in it, but she would have welcomed that feeling just now. She hoped the devastation she felt didn't show on her face. She scanned the bleachers, looking for Marc and the kids. He better not have forgotten to pick them up! And just as she had the thought, there they were—Marc standing so that she could pick him out of the group of parents. Thank God. She should have known he'd never let the kids down.

How was she ever going to tell him?

Chapter 28

Pam struggled to pull two more plastic bags out of the back of her vehicle. Once she had started packing up Stephen's clothing, she'd been surprised at the sense of purpose it gave her. She'd gotten past looking at every shirt and every tie, remembering him in them and the dinners out, the trips they had taken, the fun they had shared. Taking the first load to the nonprofit center had felt right and good and had motivated her to continue the task. Stephen would be proud of her. It was time to move on, wherever that might be.

Sacking up dress clothes was one thing, but she soon discovered that sorting through his graphic T-shirts, well-worn blue jeans, and sweatshirts was another. He had been the real Stephen in these. As driven as he'd been in his career, he had been equally driven to have fun away from work.

A hunter-green sweatshirt with an eagle in flight stitched on the front had never been worn, but he'd refused through the years to let her get rid of it.

"Mom gave it to me. God knows why. She must have thought I'd like the wildlife aspect of it," he had explained, laughing when Pam asked him about it. The love and dedication he had felt toward his mother was one of his many endearing qualities that Pam admired. Stephen's mom had died before they had married, and Pam had never met her. She wished she could have. She would have liked to thank her for raising Stephen to be such a wonderful guy. "Find a man who loves his mom, and you'll find a good husband." Somewhere she'd heard that, and Stephen had proven it to be true. She'd never doubted his love, never mistrusted him, and never questioned his faithfulness.

How often does that come along? she asked herself now, staring at the pile of clothes on the bed, knowing the thought was tinged with anger and bitterness. It was so unfair for Stephen to die. Damn it. They were having such a good life. Cancer should only happen to crappy people.

A ring tone interrupted her thoughts, and she reached into the pocket of her own sweatshirt for her cell phone. Hearing Adam's voice changed her mood and brought a smile.

"Just thinking about you, for some reason," he said. "What are you up to?"

She hesitated a second, unsure if he would appreciate what she was doing. Or at a minimum, understand. "Actually, I'm bagging up some of your dad's clothes to donate to the thrift store. Maybe someone who needs them can use them."

Adam hesitated, and Pam steeled herself for rebuff, unthinkingly running her hands through her growing pixie cut.

"Well, good. I'm sure you're right," he said. "Someone should be using them."

Pam exhaled, realizing she'd been holding her breath to hear his reaction. "I'm so glad you feel that way, Adam. It's hard to think about, I know."

"Harder on you than anyone." The care in Adam's voice had her swallowing hard before she could answer.

"Well, I don't know about that. It's hard for all of us, but it is hard to see them every day, too."

"Want some help?"

Adam's offer caught her off guard. Pam slumped down to the edge of the king-sized bed she had shared with his father for fewer years than both had hoped. She could feel the familiar ache that came with holding back tears.

"Oh, Adam. That would be great. I wish you were close enough to just run over."

"Well, I can't just run over, but I can be there tomorrow. Not much going on this weekend. I'd like to come down, if I wouldn't be in the way. Want company?"

Now the tears did fall. She had always felt that her relationship with Stephen's children was good, but she was always conscious of being the stepmom, the new woman in their dad's life. Stephen had handled parenthood and dating perfectly. Pam had never spent the night at his house when the kids were there for weekends. When they did spend time with the kids, they never overly showed affection for each other, but Stephen made it clear to Adam and Anne that he and Pam were a unit.

"I'm not sure I know how to be a stepmother or if I even want to learn how to be one," Pam had once voiced.

Stephen had just smiled at her worries. "Just be a friend."

"All the talk shows say parents shouldn't be friends."

"What do they know? Be a friend, and if and when the kids need something more from you, they'll let you know," he had said. "Trust me."

So she had strived to be a friend, and Stephen had been right. Pam had grown close to both Adam and Anne and hoped they felt the same about her. There were but a few times that the kids had indeed needed her to be more than a friend, but the memories were golden.

When Anne had an argument with her mother on the phone and felt awful about it later, she came to Pam with tears streaming down her face and asked what she should do. It still amazed Pam that, not being a mother herself, she'd handled it right, apparently. She'd urged Anne to call her mom back, after calming down, and to just tell her that she loved her. That was all she needed to do.

And when Adam broke his leg during football practice one afternoon before Stephen got home from work, Pam took him to the emergency room, calling both of his parents from the waiting room. She could still remember thinking, *This is how it feels to be a mom*. Worried. Scared for Adam to be in pain. Wanting to do more.

She had played a role in both of the children's lives. Now that they were adults, she seemed closer to them than ever, despite the loss of Stephen to connect them. Or maybe because of it. She was a link to their dad now.

The memories came flooding back as she realized Adam was waiting for an answer.

"I'd love to have you here," she said. "Maybe there are things you would want. Mostly, it would just be wonderful to see you. Just be forewarned—I'm kind of a mess."

"You're allowed," he answered solemnly. Pam knew he could probably hear the tears in her voice and was relieved when he didn't require her to answer. He had a friend who had kept a blog about her own battle against breast cancer, and he had forwarded the link to Pam when she was first diagnosed—a simple gesture that had meant the world to her. He had some inkling of what she was going through, and it helped.

"See you tomorrow," he said now, adding, "I'll bring beer."

She smiled at his parting message. Stephen would have been the one to drink the beer. They both knew that.

Chapter 29

Jessie hadn't been to the cancer center for three weeks, and it felt wonderful. Thursdays were just Thursdays again. She had finished her six chemo treatments. Done were the three hours of sitting in the black plastic recliner. Done were the weekly lab tests to check her blood count. Done were the painful injections. She still had a treatment once a month, but it was a short one by comparison—an hour, tops. She still saw Dr. Park once a month for a grand total of fifteen minutes, during which time he would look over her chart, ask how she was feeling, examine her breasts for any changes, joke with her about her college football team—which was his alma mater's rival—and send her on her way.

She didn't look forward to the appointments, but neither did she dread them as she once had and as others told her they did, fearful of getting bad news.

As long as she felt good—and she did—she wouldn't entertain that thought. While she still didn't seem to have her old energy level back, and there were remnants of "chemo brain," when she couldn't remember even simple details, both were symptoms of the treatments, not of cancer. The cancer hadn't hurt. She hadn't even known she had it until they told her she did. It was the cure that was tough. She didn't anticipate anything different about today's visit with Dr. Park. She was done with the disease; now she was dealing with the cure.

She actually looked forward to seeing the group again and catching up on their news. Over the course of their treatments together, they'd become friends. Details of their individual lives had emerged through casual conversations. There was so much more to each of them than being a cancer patient.

She had thought before about just stopping in on a Thursday but wondered how that would feel if she were the one sitting in a black recliner, still going through chemo, and in walks someone almost through with it—someone with hair (or fuzz, anyway), with plans for the day, with hope. So she never had. Until today.

Jessie pulled open the heavy door to the center and immediately looked to her right, expecting to see Irene in her usual chair in the corner, but the recliner was empty. Karen and Marcie were here. She hoped Pam's appointment was close to the time of hers so that they'd see each other. They had tried to schedule that once but quickly learned that requesting specific appointment times was frowned on. Perhaps there was a method to Dr. Park's day that they didn't know.

Karen looked up from her knitting and Marcie from her e-reader. Both immediately smiled and seemed genuinely happy to see her, which put Jessie at ease.

"Hey, guys, how's everything?" Jessie asked.

The two friends looked good.

"Like the hair, Karen," Jessie said. "Looks really good on you."

In her typically self-deprecating way, Karen pulled on the ear tabs, causing the white wig to move slightly left on her head. "Thanks. I wish it was more comfortable," she said. "Now that the center finally decided to turn on some heat, it's hot. Feels like I'm wearing an animal on my head. But you know that."

"Yeah, I remember," Jess said, smiling. She felt a little weird, knowing she was through wearing a wig, and these women were not. Her hair was still only a mess of brown fuzz, but it was there. It had a little more curl to it than she remembered, and while it wasn't a great style, it was better than wearing a wig. She remembered Bethany's prediction that she might wear the wig on "bad-hair days." That wasn't going to happen. No bad-hair day was that bad.

Marcie adjusted her ball cap, and Jessie could tell that under it, her head was still bald. "If I'd known you were going to be here today, I'd have worn my wig to show you," Marcie said. "I finally broke down and borrowed one."

Jessie smiled at the young woman. "What's it like?"

She was glad Marcie had decided to get a wig but wished she'd bought one for herself instead of borrowing one of those available through the center. Jessie had gotten the impression that Marcie didn't spend much money on herself, preferring to buy for her kids. A wig, in Jessie's opinion, wasn't a luxury. It was a necessity.

"Pretty much like my real hair," Marcie answered, smiling. "Only better. I wasn't going anywhere but here today, so I decided not to wear it. I'm still getting used to it, and I'm pretty comfortable in caps."

"Well, you look cute in them," Jessie said, eyeing the IV line threaded under Marcie's zip-up hoodie. "You're getting a treatment," Jessie said. "I thought you might be through." She remembered that she and Marcie had started chemo the same week.

Marcie grimaced. "Well, I saw Dr. Park a couple of weeks ago. Then Dr. Catterson. Another MRI shows more tissue that could be cancer, so they're keeping me on chemo until I have a biopsy, just in case it is. I'm a little tired of this."

Jessie was shocked and hoped it didn't show on her face or in her voice. *Being angry is better*, she thought, *for everyone*. "Well, damn it. Have they scheduled surgery?"

"Not yet. The biopsy is Monday. I guess surgery will be scheduled then, depending on what Dr. Catterson finds."

Marcie sounded so resigned. Jessie hated it. Marcie shouldn't even be here, and now this.

"I guess if the biopsy shows something, I'll have to start all over," Marcie said. "Dr. Park isn't saying much. You know how he is. 'Let's see what we're dealing with.'"

Jessie and Karen looked at each other, neither knowing what to say.

Marcie offered a small smile, wanting to ease the tension in the room.

"Marc and the kids doing okay?" Jessie asked. "If I can help with anything, I'd be happy to."

"Marc's good. Hanging in there, you know?" Marcie said. "We haven't told the kids anything. It's all so over their heads. We couldn't see scaring them until we know more. And thanks for the offer. I appreciate that. I really do, but Marc's mom is going to come over and stay for a few days, so we'll be fine. I think she's actually looking forward to it. She probably can't wait to get her hands on my messy pantry."

The women laughed, but it was a hollow sound. Karen and then Jessie were led back to exam rooms for their appointments.

Marcie settled back on the black recliner, pulling the sweatshirt a little more snugly over the plastic line leading into her chest.

While his wife sat in a cold cancer-treatment center with an IV line pumping deadly chemicals into her bloodstream, Marc sat in his boxer shorts on an orange motel-room bedspread. Washing up in the bathroom was the woman he'd been meeting for months.

What am I doing? he thought as he pulled on his socks. He didn't want to be here. He wanted to break it off. He would break it off. Today.

Until recently, he had considered these liaisons in a seedy motel room as a morale booster. But who was he kidding? He felt worse than ever. He'd never felt as if he deserved a wife like Marcie or a life like the one she had built, and he was honest enough to admit their life had been built by her. Sure, he brought home the paycheck, but she made the house a home. She made their family a family. And she'd been holding up the marriage pretty much all by herself, in addition to everything else she was going through. Cancer, for God's sake.

No more, he thought, *this is over*. It had started as a thrill, but it sickened him now. After he had pulled on his jeans and T-shirt, he turned to face the woman.

"I can't see you anymore," he said and walked out the door. Just like that. To her credit, the woman didn't say anything, nor did she try to stop him. She had known all along his wife was going through chemo. Truth be told, she probably didn't want to see him anymore either.

Ending the affair didn't make him feel any better, but Marc was resolved to try harder, to be the husband Marcie deserved and needed. Driving to the cancer center, he realized he didn't even know which hospital entrance to use. How bad was that? His wife had been going through chemo treatments for weeks, and he didn't even know where to find her. Or how she would react when he did. Marcie had been so strong through all of this, and she was going to have to be stronger, since her latest tests had shown there might be more cancer to kill. God, why hadn't he been there for her?

The hospital volunteer was kind and nonjudgmental when he asked where to find the treatment room. Still, he had been embarrassed when she had calmly explained that he was at the wrong wing, that he needed to go to the back of the hospital.

Now, parked outside the door with its designation of Cancer Treatment Center, he dreaded going in. *Well, good God*, he thought. Marcie probably felt the same way and had for months. If she could go through everything she had gone through, he could do this.

He didn't know what he expected, but at the very least, he'd thought the room would be larger. It looked as if hospital maintenance had moved boxes out of a storage room to make way for the recliners, each flanked by an IV pole and stand. Marcie was the only person there, looking so small under a thin blanket that covered her from her neck down to her tennis shoes. Her eyes widened when she looked up to see him standing in the doorway. Marc winced at the panic he saw on her face.

"Is everything okay?" she asked. "What are you doing here?"

"Everything is fine." He hoped his voice sounded normal. "Just came by to see if I could take my wife for a late lunch."

Marcie shook her head. Something wasn't right, and she knew it. "The kids are all okay? Are you sure?"

"They're in school," Marc answered. "They're fine, honey. Really. Want to go out for lunch when you're finished?" Marc motioned to the IV stand, trying to not look at the line leading from it to somewhere inside her sweatshirt. He had never even seen the spot on her chest where the port had been inserted. Once, he had noticed the bump under a T-shirt and had glanced away. He didn't want to know about it. He knew now that he had to stop ignoring the reality. This was definitely happening, and his wife was going through it alone. He wanted nothing more than to make up the last few months to her. Hopefully, she would never find out about the affair. He suspected Emily knew about it, somehow, but he had bargained on her not telling Marcie. And he was pretty sure that she hadn't. God, how he wished it had never happened. Just the thought of it now made him sick.

Marcie looked at him suspiciously, still unsure about his sudden appearance in the treatment room. "That would be wonderful," she said timidly. "But I'm going to be here for a while yet. Another hour and a half anyway. I'm sure you have things to do."

He hated the way she was letting him off so easily. He knew he could admit that he did have things to do. For one, he was already late in getting back to work after taking his early "lunch," and Marcie would accept it if he told her he did indeed need to get back. And life would just go on as usual. She wouldn't begrudge his departure. But he would, now and forever.

"Nah. Nothing is so important that it won't still be there whenever I make it back in. Let's have lunch, Marcie." He hated the pleading sound in his voice.

"Well, that would be great, if you don't might waiting." Her eyes softened as she sat up straighter in the recliner. She dropped the thin blanket to her lap, attempting to look more like just a wife and less like a patient. She handed him the remote control. "You might be able to find something better on TV. I just left it on the channel that came up when I turned it on."

Marc glanced up to the little flat-screen TV mounted to the wall on the other side of the room.

"This is good," he said, giving Marcie a grin she hadn't seen for a while. "I've always liked *Little House on the Prairie*."

One by one, he met two other women as they finished with their appointments and exited through the same door he had entered. He tried to remember their names: Jessie and Karen. He knew he would never remember which was which, but maybe Marcie would give him details later. Their warmth toward his wife was something he hadn't expected. She'd made friends here? In this horrible little room? He shouldn't have been surprised. Everyone loved Marcie, and no one more than him.

Chapter 30

Karen had read somewhere—probably in one of the many pamphlets she had picked up faithfully during the first month of treatments, before eventually realizing that they were depressing—that one of the side effects to having cancer was incessant Internet browsing. It had made her smile then, but she now realized it was true. She'd spent countless hours looking up sites on surviving breast cancer, and before that, she had researched breast lumps and learned that few are actually malignant. She'd seen diagrams of tissues, breasts after lumpectomies, breasts after mastectomies. She'd read about the possible side effects from the four drugs she was being given. She'd also linked into blogs written by others who were going through the process.

Her favorite site was a chat room that originated in England. She never entered the conversations; she simply felt a degree of relief by reading comments from women a continent away who were going through the same hell.

Yes, they seemed to have a constant runny nose. "Never go anywhere without a tissue up your sleeve."

Yes, they had a persistent sore throat. "Lemon drops help."

Yes, they had gained weight. Several blamed the extra pounds on the steroids that were administered to help battle side effects. Others said they had gained from constantly eating in an attempt to find something that tasted good. It was said that the average gain was about a stone. Karen looked it up and learned that a stone is fourteen pounds.

None complained of losing weight, which worried her. She'd lost about twelve pounds so far.

Yes, the women agreed, fatigue and lack of concentration was still an issue, even a few years after completing treatment. *Years? Oh, joy*, Karen thought.

She clung with hope to the messages about symptoms that she was experiencing too. Maybe her persistent back pain was normal, as everyone seemed to have it. Yet another web search showed breast cancer can often spread to the bones, showing up most likely in the spine. But that didn't mean it would happen to her. Her blood counts were good. Dr. Park said so. Every month.

She learned that pain in the shoulders, particularly when reclining, could be a sign that cancer had spread. She'd gone for physical therapy when the pain in her right shoulder kept her awake at night. It was better now, so it was probably nothing.

Her feet hurt so much in the mornings that she had trouble walking. Her relief on finding the same complaint in the English chat room was immense.

Now, Karen worried that she was a hypochondriac. She had to admit she'd always been a bit of one. Even in high school, when a friend mentioned having a headache, she had to bite her tongue to keep from blurting out that, yes, she had one too. Cramps? Yes, she had them too—and worse. The fact was she felt a little better knowing other women had the same complaints.

Every ache and pain filled her with fear now. She'd tried to talk to Dr. Park about it, hoping he'd reassure her. While his response wasn't what she had hoped, it helped.

"You just take good care of yourself and leave the worrying to me. That's my job. I'll let you know if there is anything you need to be worried about."

Easier said than done, she knew. But she was trying to stop the constant fretting and just get on with living. She wasn't sure she'd ever really been able to do that. She had always been a worrier. But if there was ever a time to just appreciate life, this was it.

She thought back to meeting Marcie's husband the day before. He seemed like a nice guy, even though he appeared to be overly eager to be kind to his wife. *Well*, Karen thought, *that's understandable considering the circumstances*. He'd never stopped into the green room before, but Marcie could have a long road ahead of her. His presence was better late than never, Karen guessed. Marcie had seemed okay with the idea that she might have to face another surgery and more chemo. Karen admitted to herself that she wouldn't be able to handle that, to go through everything for a second time. She hoped Marc was as good as he seemed. They were all worried about their young friend.

Karen shook her head to dispel the sad thoughts and wondered what to fix for dinner. She didn't relish the task of stopping by the market, but she also didn't think she could squeeze another decent meal out of leftovers. Jon was wonderful to say he liked having breakfast at night, and it was an easy meal to fix if there were eggs on hand. But three nights in one week? That would be pushing the limit, even with his easy temperament.

They hadn't eaten anything really unhealthy for a long time (not counting eggs three nights out of seven). *Something fried sounds good*, she thought as she pulled into the grocery store's parking lot.

She was trying to decide which sounded better, chicken or chops, as she maneuvered the unbalanced cart down the aisle, when she suddenly felt she was being watched. Looking up, she smiled tentatively at an acquaintance from the church she and Jon attended once a year or so. Maybe less. Christmas, at least.

"Karen, it's good to see you," the woman said, reaching out in what seemed to be slow motion. "Gosh, I haven't seen you in ages. How are you?" The last words seemed to drip with exaggerated concern as the woman's hand found Karen's where it rested on the cart handle. "I think of you so often," the woman continued. "You're in my prayers. And you are on the church's list of concerns, of course."

Karen fought the urge to pull her hand away. While some people expressed genuinely heartfelt concern, others could hardly veil the thought of *Thank God, it's you and not me* in their well wishes. Karen wasn't sure which it was with this woman, and she resisted the urge—just barely—to wish her problems on this near-stranger. What would she say to this woman if the roles were reversed? The same things, probably, she conceded. It was what people did.

How could she possibly explain everything that she was going through—how much stronger she felt, not just physically but emotionally as well? *What doesn't kill you makes you stronger*, she thought now. It was such a pat phrase, but she now realized it was true.

"Thank you for thinking of me," she said to the woman, offering her a genuine smile. "I'm doing great." She was surprised to realize that she meant it. Still smiling, Karen started to push her cart away, but the woman reached out and placed her hand on the side.

"I know it doesn't really help," the woman said. Karen was momentarily puzzled by the comment but listened as the woman continued. "But I went through breast cancer, too. About twenty years ago now. It doesn't seem possible that it's been that long. Some days, it seems like yesterday, and some days, it seems like it never really happened."

Chills ran down Karen's arms, and now she really didn't know what to say. "I didn't know," she said quietly.

"Most people don't. We lived in Colorado then," the woman said. "I wouldn't have mentioned it, but I want you to know that you really have been on my mind. I thought if I ever saw you, I'd tell you. There are more of us out there than most people know."

Karen thought of all the posts on websites, the various blogs that she had devoured, and her new friends in the green room. She smiled at the woman and gave her a sincere quick hug. "I'm glad you told me," she said. "It does help."

The woman smiled at her, and they each turned their carts to resume shopping.

Karen held onto the conversation as she walked through the store. She looked at the other women shoppers differently, knowing it was entirely possible that some of them had gone through this, too.

Suddenly, she felt that everything was going to be okay. She hadn't allowed herself to think that way for months. Maybe the positive attitudes of the other women—on the Internet, in the green room, even in the grocery store—were rubbing off on her. *Pam, Jessie, Marcie, and Irene would be proud of me*, she thought, and she realized with a grin that she was feeling pretty proud of herself, too.

Chapter 31

Pam set her coffee mug on the counter and smiled as the doorbell chimed. Adam was here, as promised, at a few minutes after nine on Saturday morning. Pam hadn't doubted that he would come. He was so like his dad—dependable, once a plan was in place. If he said he'd do something, he would. Just like his father.

Stephen had been as true to his word as a man could be; he just hadn't given his word freely, and making plans in advance of a day or so was nearly unheard of during their courtship and marriage. It had frustrated Pam until she had consciously decided to accept this as an endearing aspect to his personality, instead of one that drove her crazy. Eventually, she'd just made her own plans and told them to Stephen. They had either fit with his or not. She'd learned through the years that having a decision made was something of a touchstone for him. He could go from that point, one way or another. It was the getting there that had been tough for him. They had figured it out through the years, and it had worked for them.

Pam hoped her own decision to sell their house was going to be acceptable to both Adam and Anne. They hadn't lived there full time, that was true, but their father had, and she had taken that into consideration when she made her decision. His children had spent long weekends with them, and it had always been fun. The house was another link to Stephen that was being broken. But she needed to find something she could more easily manage, financially and emotionally. She hoped they would understand.

The first step toward moving had been to clean out closets and dressers. She had sorted out most of his clothes, but the closet and drawers were far from empty. She knew going through his dad's belongings wasn't going to be easy for Adam or for her either. But if they looked at it as a necessary step toward a larger one, it would help.

Instead of beer, Adam had come bearing giant cups of iced coffee, a love they had in common, and they sat on the deck, looking out over the pasture beyond. Neither was eager to start on the project.

"You're going to miss this," Adam said. "Sure you want to move?"

Pam turned from looking at his profile, so like his father's, to share his view. The lone horse meandered through the short grass. "I will," she admitted. "And yes, Adam. I am sure."

The bed in the guestroom was heaped with Stephen's casual clothes. These had ended up in the pile Pam had dubbed the "give-away" rather than the "donate" stack. Those items had already gone to the nonprofit organization. Dressy clothes weren't Adam's thing. *Plus*, she thought, *what he* *doesn't know is already gone he can't miss.* But maybe there were items in the give-away stack that he would want.

"I remember his wearing this," Adam said, picking up a dark-blue flannel shirt. "He liked it."

"He did," Pam answered.

Adam laid it aside, starting a new pile. He added another shirt and then a sweatshirt. He picked up the one with the embroidered eagle on the front and laughed, giving Pam a quizzical look. "Please tell me Dad never wore this."

Pam laughed. "Your grandmother gave it to him. And no, he never wore it, but he couldn't bring himself to get rid of it either. I can't imagine that she ever really thought he would wear it. Maybe she meant it as a joke."

The sweatshirt went on top of the pile that Pam now thought of as Adam's "keep" pile, along with a pair of nylon parachute pants, a Kansas University long-sleeved T-shirt, a fleece jacket, and another flannel shirt.

Then, to her surprise, Adam picked up the entire pile in his arms and dropped it back on top of the original stack of clothes. "You know, I think I just want to remember these things but not have them," he said. "It's too hard. And they'll just be in my closet for years, until someday, someone else will have to go through them and wonder about them. Just give it all way, Pam."

The mood had grown somber. These were Stephen's things, and he was gone. His scent—a mixture of Zest soap, aftershave, and perspiration—still clung to some of the clothing.

Pam punched Adam playfully on the arm, trying to lighten the mood before they were both in tears. "You just don't want anyone thinking you've ever worn a sweatshirt with an eagle on it," she said with a loving grin.

Adam nodded and gave Pam a quick hug. He understood her reason for cleaning out his dad's closet and even for selling the house. But he hoped the reasons she'd given him were the only ones. He hoped she was okay.

Chapter 32

Marcie debated about making a pot of real coffee. She'd switched to decaf years ago on the advice of her gynecologist, who had told her that caffeine might be contributing to the fibroid cysts in her breasts. Well, she didn't worry about cysts anymore. Add that to the plus column, because, so far, the minuses were winning.

Lack of energy was one of those minuses. Still, she knew the laundry wasn't going to do itself. The other option was to watch yet another morning talk show, where they showed "easy, healthy recipes to make tonight" with ingredients she couldn't find in any of the three local grocery stores. And even if she did make a new dish, her kids wouldn't touch it. Laundry seemed the more appealing choice.

Still, she wondered, *who would have thought gathering up dirty clothes would be such a daunting task?* The kids' rooms were easy. Ellie and Madi shared a pink room, with twin beds covered in matching pastel spreads. The girls were pretty good at putting their clothes into the white wicker hampers beside the closet. Pretty good but not great, although they were learning. They had favorite outfits, and they were figuring out that if the tops and tights didn't get put into the dirty clothes bag, the garments wouldn't magically reappear in their dressers.

Christopher wasn't as tidy or observant. Marcie often thought he'd be content to wear the same shirt daily until it eventually disintegrated. He'd actually been known to turn a favorite sports jersey inside out to get one more day of wear out of it. Keeping him in clean clothes was a daily challenge.

Marcie grabbed the bags out of the girls' hampers and upended them on the laundry room floor. She made a quick trip through Chris's room, gathering up jeans, sweatshirts, socks, and underwear, and added them to the heap. Everything white or light-colored went into the washer; darks could wait, so she pushed them aside with her foot to make a path out of the room.

Marcie thought others might find it strange, but the laundry room was actually one of her favorite rooms in the house, mostly because she had made it her own. She had painted the walls lemon yellow and covered the small window with a woven shade of soft summer colors. It was a cheerful room, probably the most cheerful in the house. Marc had no interest in it; in fact, he likely couldn't have told someone the color of the walls or if there even was a window there.

Marcie loved every room of their home; truly she did. She just wished it was more uniquely theirs. The house was situated on one side of a cul-de-sac in a newer development. The exteriors of the homes were all different. Some had small porches, and a few had decorative window shutters. The front doors were painted in various colors. Few would call them cookie-cutter homes, but Marcie knew from the occasional neighborhood get-togethers that they all had nearly identical floor plans. The builder may have flipped the plan, moved the kitchen, or changed a bathroom here and there, but mostly they were the same.

That's okay, Marcie thought. With their track record, she knew they weren't going to live here forever. She and Marc both longed to buy a few acres on the edge of town, eventually. Marcie wanted to garden, not vegetables as much as flowers. Marc just wanted space. Period. As it was, if she raised the blinds at her kitchen sink, she'd be looking into the kitchen of the house next door.

Still, it was a nice place to call home. While there were boxes stacked in the garage still to unpack, she'd gotten the bulk of it done before her diagnosis and treatment. The kids loved it here. The neighborhood was filled with other young families, and the well-used backyards teemed with trampolines, brightly colored playhouses, and countless toys. She didn't have any reason to complain.

While she waited for the coffee to finish brewing, she went to the master bedroom and gathered the bed linens and Marc's work shirts. She carried the bulky load into the laundry room, using her chin to keep it all balanced.

She later wondered if she hadn't done that—if she hadn't decided to change the sheets or to do laundry at all—if she might not have ever smelled the unfamiliar perfume on her husband's shirt.

Marcie sat down on a stool at the folding table. She felt lightheaded, her mind fuzzy. She picked up the shirt again, breathing in the strong scent. She had stopped wearing any perfume years ago and certainly never considered putting it on now. The drugs pumped into her veins during chemo gave her enough of a headache, and she never knew which odors would suddenly have her feeling nauseated and running for the bathroom.

She tried to think of a reasonable explanation as to why his shirt would smell this strongly of perfume. A coworker, maybe? Some middle-aged woman who really poured it on until the whole office reeked? Marc would have some answer, some good reason, if she confronted him. His reply would make her look and sound like a pathetic housewife, bored with her own life and suspicious of her husband. True, with three little kids and now going through chemo, she wasn't the energetic woman she had once been or as concerned about her appearance, but she had never doubted Marc's fidelity. Until now.

She was shocked at how quickly her mind went to the idea of divorce and whether or not she'd ever have another man in her life. What man in his right mind would want a woman who had had a breast removed? Maybe both breasts, when this was all said and done. She didn't know if that was going to happen yet, but it seemed like a good possibility. What man would want a woman with the baggage of exorbitant medical bills? One who also had three young children?

And would she even be around to ponder the decision of divorce anyway?

She felt sick and knew the thoughts weren't good for her, mentally or physically.

Maybe there was a good reason for the perfume. Maybe she was just imagining things. Maybe she wouldn't even bring it up. It would be easy to just throw the shirt in the laundry and wash away the incriminating evidence. She would never mention it, and they would go on with their lives. Everything had been so good lately. Marc was more caring and considerate than he had been in years. He was even taking more interest in the kids, playing with them after supper, helping to get them into baths and then to bed.

Was she willing to lose all of that, everything she had, because of a stinky shirt?

Was there a reason he was suddenly being so attentive to her and the kids?

Her head hurt. She was tired of thinking. Tired of wondering. Tired of holding back tears. Just tired, in general.

Without thinking, she stuffed the offending shirt into the washer, added detergent, and hit the start button.

She didn't know what she was going to do or what she wanted to do. Confront Marc? Let it go but pay more attention to his whereabouts?

She knew only one thing for certain: she didn't have the energy to deal with it right now.

Chapter 33

"Pam!" Jessie couldn't believe the joy she felt at seeing her friend. Outside of doctors and nurses, Pam was the first person Jessie had met when she started this whole process, and she had steered Jessie through that first morning of chemotherapy when she'd been scared out of her mind, too frightened actually to even admit it. Jessie still remembered staring at the poster promoting the survivors' walk as she waited to be hooked up to the IV stand, reading and rereading the words and growing more anxious by the moment.

Pam was her anchor, not to the past and really not even to the present but to the future, to hope that life could—would—someday return to some degree of normal.

Jessie had seen Pam only a handful of times since finishing chemo, always in the green room with the other women. She'd enjoyed their conversations; both loved the outdoors, iced coffee, fashion magazines, animals, and music. She had carried Pam's handwritten phone number in her purse for the past six months, but she hadn't called her. She wasn't sure why not.

"Oh, my gosh. It is so good to see you." Jessie hugged her friend to her and then pulled away suddenly. There was no good reason for Pam to be here.

Pam laughed and tucked her short blonde hair behind her ears. "It's great to see you, too. You're looking good. Love the hair. Loved the wig but really love the hair." She reached up and fluffed Jessie's short brown bob.

Before her hair grew back, Jessie swore she would never, ever complain about it again. She'd always had thin, fine hair. A family trait, unfortunately. Along with breast cancer, apparently. She told herself that if and when she had hair again, it would be wonderful—thin, fine, and all. That didn't last long. When it had grown enough to resemble some sort of style, she made her first appointment with a stylist in almost a year.

She shared all of this with Pam. "I guess I thought when I told the stylist that I wanted some shape to what little hair I had that she could make it longer."

Pam laughed. She was so happy to see that Jessie had handled the chemo without it stealing away her spunk. "It's cute," Pam said. "Pixie-ish. That's all the rage, you know. Look at all the movie stars who are cutting off their long hair for a short style. It's darling."

"Yeah, well. I don't look like a movie star," Jessie said, grinning at Pam.

"You're just as cute." Pam gave her friend a quick hug. "It'll keep growing. And it does have a style. Seriously. Plus, its loads thicker, isn't it?"

"It is." Jessie nodded. "No complaining about bad-hair days. I have to remember that I promised myself that."

Pam smiled. All of the women had made that promise. "And you're feeling good?" Pam asked.

"I am," Jessie answered. She felt buoyed by the reconnection and in what she hoped were better circumstances.

A rush of gratitude surprised her. "I've thought of you so often. I'm sorry I haven't called."

Pam just laughed again. "Hey, no problem. I'm so glad everything is good with you. All through?"

"I am," Jessie answered again, realizing she sounded like a giddy teenager, but her mood had just improved by giant leaps. Seeing Pam again made her realize just how far she had come, how much she had endured, and how much stronger she was. "Well, through with the weekly treatments anyway. I still get one drug every third Thursday and have to see Dr. Park once a month. Plus, I need to schedule my final heart echo, but the results have all been good. So I'm *almost* done. Now I just need to get some energy back into my life. But it's getting there."

Jessie looked closer at her friend, the one who seemed to all of the other women to have it more together than any of them. She realized Pam looked drawn. She thought back to the last time she had seen her. It was after an appointment with the oncologist. That had been a month ago, and they had just passed in the hallway without time to visit.

"Are *you* okay?" she asked. "You look tired, Pam."

"Oh, you know. Ups and downs." Pam had never talked much about herself, always turning the conversation to one of the others.

Jessie refused to let her off so easily. "So. What are the ups and what are the downs?" They were standing in the hallway, with exam and consultation rooms spaced on both sides. The doors were shut, meaning patients were either with Dr. Park or waiting to see him.

Pam shrugged. "Well, depends on how you look at it, I guess. I've been cleaning out Stephen's clothing, packing them up to donate or discard. That's kind of hard, but it feels good at the same time. Adam came to help."

Jessie had finally learned that Pam had lost her husband to prostate cancer just as she was going through her own treatments. God, that had to have been so hard. Jessie couldn't imagine. Pam talked about her stepchildren often, and Jessie knew they were close. She was glad. Pam would have been a great mom. No, she *was* a great mom.

"How was that? Having Adam there? Make it easier or harder?"

"Oh, easier. Definitely. Not that it wasn't still hard," Pam said. "It's hard for Adam too, but he was supportive, and we had some laughs. That helped. I wish he lived closer. I guess a couple of hours isn't so far away. And I'm so glad that he's stayed in touch—kept me a member of the family."

Jessie thought of her own three children, now almost grown. They all lived nearby and she and Greg enjoyed having them close. Especially now. She was happy for Pam and glad that Stephen's son had driven down to see her, regardless of the reason. That had to have been a boost for her.

"I'm sure it was hard for both of you, going through the clothes," Jessie said.

Pam thought of the eagle sweatshirt and smiled to herself. "It was good to clear some of that stuff out, finally. Hopefully, someone else will be able to use it. I did keep a few things—for sentimental reasons, I guess. I need to go through all of my clothes, too. Maybe I'll start this weekend. What is it they say? If you haven't worn it in a year, get rid of it. How about ten years? Honestly, I have clothes that old."

"We all do." Jessie looked down at the "uniform" she had adopted for chemo sessions. "This top is probably that old. It's comfy, though, like an old friend. I'll probably keep it until it is in shreds. Then maybe I'll make a pillow out of it and keep it around a little longer."

Pam laughed. "The pink fleece you wore for almost every single chemo treatment? I think you should have a ceremony and burn it."

Jessie laughed with her. "I don't know. It's been with me through an awful lot of life." She looked at her friend. Pam still hadn't answered her question of how she was doing.

Pam suddenly seemed uncomfortable. She had a look of sorrow in her eyes, and Jessie hated it—hated what she knew was likely true. Her friend suddenly looked on the edge of tears, her pale face blotchy. Jessie had been going on and on about how great she was doing without thinking that the same might not be true for Pam. She looked on the verge of collapse, and Jessie didn't want to know the reason. For Pam and for herself. Whatever was causing tears to well up in her friend's eyes, it couldn't be anything good.

"Pam?" Jessie's voice came out as barely a whisper. "What's up?"

Chapter 34

Karen understood. Really, she did. If she owned the business, she'd want someone more dependable than a worker who might call in sick on any given morning, leave before closing time on any given afternoon, and require every Thursday off. Still, it hurt. She loved her job. Her coworkers were her friends. Her only friends, really, unless you counted the girls from the green room. She was going to be lost without them.

She also understood that she wasn't really being let go. Her boss was offering her a part-time position—with less responsibility, less pay. It felt like a token offer; let's give the cancer survivor a spot. Can't fire her. Could be sued for that.

Karen hated the way her mind was going. Mr. Parsons didn't think any of those things. At least, she didn't think so. No, he needed to know the department manager was going to be there every day, putting out fires when they started, not showing up days down the road when the place was going up in flames. Her mind understood that. She wasn't so sure about her heart.

She forced a smile, letting her boss off the hook. "I appreciate your kindness and your patience with everything that I've had going on," she said. "I'm sorry that I've had to miss so many days. You've been very understanding, but I think it's time to look for a new job."

Looking back now, she told herself that he had grimaced because he was disappointed in her decision and that it wasn't relief she saw in his eyes and in the tight smile he gave her before shaking hands, thanking her for everything, and wishing her well.

Now she sat at the kitchen table with the newspaper classified ads spread before her. Most of the jobs, many in the health care field, weren't something she felt she could do, even if she had been qualified.

Maybe she could go back to school. She'd taken a few courses at the local college in the early years of their marriage, after the baby died, when she'd felt lost and disconnected from everyone. She had hated the classes and had felt so much older than the other students, even though they were the same age. She'd gone through too much and had been forced to grow up too quickly; there was no going back.

Now, she would be much older than most of the other students, but college was something to think about. Taking a course or two might give her connections that would lead to a new career path. She and Jon certainly didn't have any extra money for college, but she'd heard about scholarships for nontraditional students. If that classification didn't include her, she didn't know what did. Maybe there were special scholarships for fifty-year-old cancer victims.

Her mood was dark; she knew that. Tough. She was allowed.

The steps she'd taken in the attempt to be a more positive person were slipping away. She could actually feel the drain on her attitude that came from no longer having somewhere to go every morning—other than Thursdays, when her trip was to the green room.

Karen knew—from articles she'd read, the websites, chat rooms she had visited, and from personal observation—that attitude had a lot to do with how well you handled chemo. She needed to get on a happier path.

She circled one ad for a "part-time administrative assistant in a fast-paced office." She wondered how fast-paced it could be if they only needed an administrative assistant part-time. Still, it sounded good. She had always liked the cleanliness of office work, the completion of tasks, the filing away of work when it was finished.

She'd be off her feet, and that was a big plus. Her feet still hurt from the aftereffects of chemo. The tingling in her fingers and toes that had lasted for weeks had been bad enough, but now she had actual pain in her feet, so much so that walking from the bed to the bathroom every morning was a dreaded trip. Dr. Park had told her it would subside with time.

"Massage them when you can," he said. "Putting them on an ice pack or rolling them on a frozen water bottle in the evenings will help too."

She had done all of that, and it had helped, but still they hurt. The part-time job probably didn't offer health insurance, but she hadn't had that in her old job either. Fortunately, Jon's work offered family policies, and while it wasn't cheap, it was there. So far, the premiums hadn't increased, nor had the policy been canceled after Jon's injury and her diagnosis and costly treatments. That was a steady worry. Karen realized she had probably acted impulsively in turning down the demotion. Still, her feeling of self-worth would certainly have suffered if she'd accepted it. She didn't want to go backward.

I'll find something, she thought. She tore out the small ad for office help and placed it on top of the computer keyboard. She'd spruce up her résumé, check with her references to see if they would still put in a good word for her, and send off an application in the morning.

They'd be darn lucky to get me, she thought.

Chapter 35

Pam always enjoyed getting her mail. In fact, it had become a joke with friends and family. "No one reads all of their junk mail like Pam does," they teased. If she admitted it, it was the quiet time of sitting down with a cup of coffee to see what was going on in the world that she enjoyed. But yes, she did enjoy junk mail—or rather, she enjoyed critiquing it. From her job, which encompassed working closely with the marketing department, she knew someone, somewhere, had typed those words, played with graphics until he got the look he wanted, worked with a printer to check color and font options, and likely harassed the mailer to make sure it had gone out on schedule.

She enjoyed seeing if the layout and words supported each other and got the message out in the best light. In the past, she'd been able to come up with ideas for the flyers, brochures, and letters, which she felt were an improvement, but technology had reached a point that she now wondered, *How did they do that?* She considered the activity as a brain challenge, and her brain could use a few challenges these days.

The big older house that she and Stephen had so lovingly made into a home was now on the market and the subject of one of those shiny colorful flyers. As she turned it over and over in her hand, Pam had to admit that, no, she could not have done a better job than whoever had designed it. The photos made the house look even better than it did, and that was saying something. It was a beautiful home. The real estate agent assured her it would be a quick sale. "Just the grounds alone will thrill buyers," he had said. Pam knew he hoped to encourage her, but his words had only made her sadder.

"Yeah," she said aloud to herself, after the agent left. "Someone else will have a glass of wine on my patio. Someone else will enjoy my walk-in shower and my state-of-the-art kitchen. I just hope they'll give an occasional apple to Socks." Socks was the name she had given the horse in the neighboring pasture.

"That's not very original," she recalled Stephen saying. "I wonder how many cats and dogs and horses with white on their legs end up being named Socks."

"Fitting, though," she had argued, and they had laughed about it.

She truly did hope the new owners, whoever they might be (and she honestly hoped she wouldn't meet them, so she wouldn't have to imagine them in *her* kitchen, *her* bedroom) would give Socks an occasional treat. She would expect it. She hated to think of the horse missing her.

She tossed the colorful brochure into the trash. She didn't have to see the glossy photos to know it was a beautiful home. Her home. Well, not for long. She'd been lucky to find a two-bedroom condo in a newer part of town and was going to go ahead and move before the house sold.

Financially risky, she knew, but she'd come this far and was ready to move on.

Once she'd started cleaning out closets, it had seemed counterproductive to put anything back in them. Then it had seemed sad to live in such an empty house. One thing had led to another, and now she was selling and moving, before she'd had time to get used to the idea.

Surprisingly to her, Adam and Anne had been great about her decision to sell the house.

"I know you have lots of good memories there," Anne had said when Pam finally got up the nerve to call and tell her of the plans. "But there are some hard ones, too. I think moving is a great idea. It's exciting. I'm happy for you."

Adam had pretty much said the same thing the day he'd help her pack up their dad's clothing. "Starting over is always scary," he had told her, "but it can be fun, too. Go for it."

Beneath her arguments for moving and their encouragements for the change was her unspoken worry that leaving the house they had all shared with Stephen would break the bond she had with his children.

Anne had alleviated those fears. "Just be sure there's room for us wherever you go," she had said.

Pam had to swallow the lump in her throat before answering. "Absolutely."

It was silly, she supposed, that selling the house had put her in such a funk. It was the best thing, the right thing. And the kids weren't going to disappear after all. She was so glad about that. Still, it hurt. She hoped that somehow, someday, the condo would feel like home.

She worked at fighting the thought that cancer had taken enough away from her—Stephen, her familiar body, her energy, and now her home. She was relieved that it wasn't taking away her family as well.

Chapter 36

Their kids gave Greg and Jessie tickets to a country-music concert, along with a prepaid hotel room, for their anniversary. They knew how much their parents had enjoyed attending concerts before the cancer diagnosis. It was such a thoughtful gift and one they had obviously been planning for a while.

What they didn't know, Jessie thought, as she tried to feign excitement over the gift, was that she no longer relished the idea of crowds, or loud music, or bright lights, or the task of finding a parking spot at the arena. It was all too much.

While she could go without a wig now and did much of the time, she wouldn't want to be in a crowd with her short, fuzzy hair. But the wig would be too hot; plus, there was always the worry of it falling off. And she avoided crowds, as she didn't want to be bumped by strangers. Her incisions and underarms were still sensitive.

Headaches didn't seem to be a side effect to chemo, according to Dr. Park or any of the websites she had checked, but she had them. As did the other women in the green room. Attending a concert, with its loud, throbbing music and bright, flashing lights wouldn't help.

The kids didn't know all of this. She kept the daily challenges and changes to herself. *What good would it have done to tell them?* she thought. They had worried enough through the past few months.

Greg, however, understood. While thanking their children for the thoughtful gift, he suggested they use the hotel room gift card and skip the concert . . . this year.

"We're busy people, you know," he had laughed. "Can we have a rain check on a concert? We may not get out of the hotel room."

His casual and joking manner hadn't fooled anyone, but the kids had obliged, saying they'd make the same offer for the next year.

Instead, Jessie invited them all for a cookout to celebrate the anniversary, and, to her surprise, all three accepted.

After gorging themselves on hamburgers and brats off the grill, potato salad, and baked beans, followed by a chocolate cake in honor of the occasion, they had all crashed in the living room. Jessie had to grin at the antics of Matthew and Libby, who squabbled over which one should have the overstuffed chair. Hunter grabbed a pillow from the sofa and sprawled across the carpet.

None of them had brought their "significant other," although Jessie had told them that doing so would be okay. She was glad now that they hadn't. It was like having young children again, and she loved it.

Greg flipped through the TV channels before deciding to leave it on a country-music show. Jessie hoped the kids could get a refund for the tickets to the upcoming concert, but this was better. She felt guilty turning the gift down, but it just wasn't possible. Not right now. More than likely the kids would sell the tickets on the Internet for a profit. She hoped so.

"Ah, this is nice," Jessie said, as they all nestled down. The kids grabbed knitted throws out of a basket, and she wondered who would be the first to fall asleep. "We can lounge in our own living room wearing sweatpants and socks."

"I know I'm glad I wore sweatpants," Hunter said. "I'm stuffed. Good meal, Mom."

Jessie smiled. She was so happy to have them all at home. It was a rare occasion.

All five of them were sleepy and relaxed in the comfort of each other as the music played in the background. As the televised concert came to an end, the audience stood, screaming for more, and raising lighted cell phones in tribute.

"Remember the old days when we would raise lighters?" Greg said, smiling at his wife.

Jessie grinned. They had gone to several concerts through the years. In fact, Greg had proposed at one of those.

"Yes, I remember," she said, giving Greg a warm smile. She looked wistfully at the televised concert. "Can you imagine an entire room full of people giving you a standing ovation? Raising a light to honor you? That must be an amazing feeling!"

She caught a look that passed between Matthew and Hunter. Then she fought back tears when, as if by plan, the three kids and Greg all stood, holding their lighted cell phones high in the room.

"Here's to you, Mom," Libby said. "We're proud of you."

Then the tears did fall.

Chapter 37

Dr. Susan Catterson typically saw twenty or so women a day, except on Wednesdays, when she scheduled surgeries. The Breast Center had a thriving practice. The patient load had doubled in the five years since she had joined the group. At age forty-one, Susan was a highly regarded physician and surgeon, specializing in treatments of breast cancer.

Occasionally, though not often enough for her, she was able to tell a patient that a biopsy showed the lump was benign. When she couldn't give that diagnosis, she tried to temper the bad news—"Yes; it is cancer"—with better news: "It can be treated." She knew that acceptance of both the bad news and the words of hope were, understandably, often slow in coming.

"Cancer is never a good thing. Never," she would tell her patients. "But there *are* treatments, unlike many diseases where there are not."

By the time the women were recommended to Dr. Catterson, they had likely already had a mammogram, a diagnostic mammogram, a sonogram, and possibly an MRI. A biopsy was the final step before surgery. They were holding on to hope by a thinning thread.

Standing at the computer station in the hallway, Dr. Catterson studied the report on the patient waiting in the exam room. Barbara Burnett. Age forty-none. Five foot five. Weight, 158. A little overweight but not obese. A history of breast cancer in the family. A lump in one breast she'd discovered by self-exam and confirmed by a mammogram. An MRI had exposed a second lump in the same breast. Both diagnosed as "highly suspicious."

Straightening her lavender lab coat, Dr. Catterson took a deep breath and stood for a moment outside the exam room. This was the hardest part to her days. Another woman was waiting. Another woman was about to have her life altered by what Dr. Catterson would have to tell her.

She quietly opened the door and smiled at the woman lying on the exam table. "Barbara? Hi. I'm Dr. Catterson," she said, lightly touching the woman's shoulder through the thin, disposable gown. "You've met Jenny, I see." Her nurse stood beside the table in the dimly lit room, holding on to the patient's hand.

"I have," Barbara said, glancing up at the nurse and never relinquishing the hold on her hand. "She's been wonderful." Her voice was soft, and Dr. Catterson could see the fear in her eyes.

"We're going to take some tissue from each of the lumps and send that to the lab for diagnosis." Dr. Catterson kept her voice professional, both from years of practice at distancing herself from patients and because she knew that is what they wanted and needed. Someone else was in charge. No decisions to make here. Not yet. "You're breast has been numbed," she continued, "and

I'm using a device that injects directly into the lump, collects tissue, and extracts. It is all very quick, but I won't tell you it doesn't hurt. It does, but it's over in just seconds. Okay?"

Barbara's "okay" was but a whisper. Jenny squeezed her hand and asked who was with her today, just as Dr. Catterson injected the first probe.

"My husband. He's in the waiting room. Oh. Oh. That does hurt." Barbara's grip on the nurse's hand tightened.

Dr. Catterson gave Barbara a comforting smile. "One down. You're doing great."

Jenny returned the squeeze. "I think I know which husband is yours," she said, hoping to distract her patient. "Red shirt? He was on his phone when I glanced out. Does he play games on it?"

Barbara relaxed a bit and smiled up at the nurse. "That would be him, yes, but he was probably texting the kids or reading. I'm the one who plays games on the phone. Too many."

The second probe was inserted and quickly extracted.

"Oh, God. That really hurts." Barbara gave the doctor an accusatory look.

Dr. Catterson was used to that. "I know it does. But we're done, and we'll let you get dressed. When you're finished, go back to the room you were in first. Jenny will show you the way. We'll discuss your surgical options and the choice of an oncologist."

Barbara's eyes widened. Hope visibly left her expression; only the fear remained. "It's cancer?" Her voice was barely audible.

Dr. Catterson squeezed her arm, rearranging the exam gown over Barb's shoulder. This moment, for Barbara and the thousands of women who faced the same diagnosis, would forever be frozen in time. The date would be seared into their history, along with marriage anniversaries and their children's birth dates. A turning point in life. A moment that separated what came before and what was to come.

The tissue biopsy would reveal important aspects of the tumors, but Dr. Catterson was confident, sadly, of the diagnosis without it.

Her voice was strong. "I think so. Yes."

Chapter 38

Dr. Nathan Park sat again at the long wooden desk that the Cancer Center staff had cleared for him to work. He liked his work as an oncologist and looked forward to these monthly visits to the satellite center. It was good to get away from his office adjacent to a metropolitan hospital and visit a facility where the staff and patients, if they didn't already know each other, quickly became familiar during the course of treatment. That didn't always happen, of course. Some of those dealing with the onslaught of treatments, insurance forms, privacy, and next-of-kin documents opted to keep to themselves. But a group of women currently going through treatment seemed to have forged a bond.

He glanced up through the sliding glass window in front of the desk usually manned by the center's director, as the door opened, and one of his patients walked in. She looked immediately to her right, and he surmised she was looking for the other women she'd met while undergoing treatment. But she was the first to arrive. The recliners were empty; the flat screen TV attached to the opposite wall was off. He smiled at her through the glass. She smiled back, raising one hand in a timid wave.

He wasn't a friend. He understood that. If anything, he was likely viewed as a necessary adversary. He was the one who ordered what toxins would be pumped into their veins. He was the one who could give them wonderful news or a fatal diagnosis. Still, he liked to think he dispensed hope as well. They depended on him, trusted him to make lifesaving decisions for them in a world that was suddenly foreign and threatening. He took that trust seriously.

Another woman came through the front door and immediately hugged the earlier arrival. Dr. Park could see they were genuinely happy to see each other, and he enjoyed watching their interaction.

These women, the Thursday morning group, referred to the treatment area as "the green room"—he had heard that from the staff—and they seemed to pull strength and encouragement from each other. He wondered how far the connection went, and if it continued outside of the center. He had learned through nearly twenty years of medical practice that cancer was something most patients learned to tackle on their own, with the help of only family and the closest of friends. Casual acquaintances and friends on the fringe weren't likely to want the burden. He suspected that once these women were finished with their chemo, they would likely go their separate ways, more than happy to put this time behind them. They might think of each other occasionally, maybe exchange Christmas cards. He also suspected, though, that if one of them needed someone to talk to at two in the morning, any one of the group would be available at a moment's notice. *It's an intriguing and fascinating connection*, he thought, *how a crisis can create such strong bonds.*

Dr. Park scanned the day's computer-generated schedule, filled with appointments from 8:30 a.m. until 4:30 p.m. He glanced up as the door opened again and recognized Pam, who seemed to be the glue of this particular group. She was finished with chemo, surgery, and radiation and was on hormones for five years. He would continue to see her for checkups during that time. He was hopeful about her prognosis and marveled at her empathy for the other women undergoing treatment. He saw Pam now only every three months for routine exams, and whenever he did, she always made time to visit with the staff and other patients. It was easy to see why the other women admired her. But there was an air of sadness about her, though Dr. Park didn't know the source. In his mind, Pam deserved to be happy for many reasons, not the least being the way she genuinely cared about others.

Jessie entered the room with a whoosh of fresh air, as if in a hurry. She was finished with what he knew the women called "the big chemo" and was on a kinder drug for a year. She had shown a determined attitude toward her diagnosis and life in general since her treatments had started. She seemed the closest emotionally to Pam and appeared less patient with some of the other women. A realist, he decided. She had likely seen a diagnosis of breast cancer as an insult, something she would defeat. It was an attitude that did help fight the disease, he knew. Anger fueled her determination, and that had served her well.

Pam and Jessie hugged one another. Neither of the women was wearing a wig today, which made him smile.

He watched as Pam and Jessie turned to the other two women, Karen and Marcie, who had entered the center. The four women greeted each other warmly.

Karen was wearing a white page-boy wig. *It makes her look older*, Dr. Park thought, *but there must be a reason why she selected it*. Marcie also had on a wig, something new since he'd last seen her. It was long and dark brown, much like he remembered her hair as being, but the way it sat on her head was a giveaway, at least to him. He spent his days surrounded by people, mostly women, in wigs and could spot them immediately. *Marcie made a good choice*, he thought, smiling at himself for giving so much thought to his patients' hair. But he knew the way in which they regarded themselves played a huge part in how well they handled chemo.

He knew all of the patients he would see today, with the exception of one, prior to their starting treatment, when they still had their natural hair. He had seen them again as the hair started to thin and then in their assortments of wigs, scarves, and hats. Or bald. Now, he was seeing a few of them with their own hair again. He liked this phase best.

His new patient, his first for the long day, was a woman named Barbara Burnett. The chart showed she would start chemo today in the effort to shrink two tumors in her right breast prior to surgery. She'd been diagnosed only a week ago, and Dr. Park knew she would still be in shock and frightened. Rightfully so. No amount of counseling or reading up on the subject of breast cancer and chemo could truly prepare one for what was ahead. Even he, a respected oncologist, didn't know how her body would react to the extremely strong drugs. No one did. Every patient handled it differently, both physically and emotionally.

Dr. Park had noticed Barbara when she'd entered the center, accompanied by a man he assumed was her husband. The man looked almost as ill and uncomfortable as his wife. Dr. Park watched from his makeshift office behind the glassed window as the nurse visited with them. He could tell they didn't want small talk, and the nurse walked beside Barbara down the hallway to an exam room.

Barbara looked back quickly at her husband, who remained seated. They had evidently discussed this beforehand. Barbara wanted to face the oncologist alone. That wasn't unusual, although Dr. Park always appreciated seeing first-time patients who were accompanied by a family member or a close friend. In his experience, patients often nodded numbly as he detailed their treatment plan, while husbands, daughters, sisters, and close friends asked detailed questions. And took notes.

Dr. Park entered the exam room and introduced himself. He knew a significant amount of information about Barbara from the medical chart forwarded from Dr. Catterson's office. Barbara had been told the result of the biopsies: malignant.

When he pushed open the exam room door, Barbara turned to give him an apprehensive smile. She sat on the edge of the exam table in a paper gown open at the front, clutching her purse on her lap. Dr. Park tried to put her at ease, knowing it was pointless but nevertheless wanting Barbara to view him as a partner in all of this. He asked about her family and her hobbies and was interested to learn she was an amateur photographer, something they had in common. She promised to bring in some of her photos for him to see.

Dr. Park thought Barbara was a little calmer by the time he examined her breasts and then detailed the course of her treatment—the drugs she would receive, the frequency, and possible side effects to expect—although she remained quiet and tense. She was smart enough to know that he was trying to put her at ease.

He knew from his years of caring for cancer patients that Barbara would find some common ground with the staff and the other patients over the course of treatment. They would find some topic for conversation, some reason to joke with each other. But now was not the time.

"The nurse will be in to take your vital signs and draw blood," he said, finished with his examination. "That gives us a baseline to check how the drugs are affecting you. The nurse will also go over all of the chemicals you'll be receiving and explain possible side effects. Do you have any questions?"

"I don't think so," Barbara answered.

"It's a lot to take in, I know," he said, squeezing her hand. "Write down any questions you have, and I'll do my best to answer them the next time I see you, okay?"

Dr. Park could tell the tears were close as Barbara smiled and thanked him, a response that, even now, never failed to surprise him.

Jessie was his next appointment, and he always enjoyed visiting with her. Doctors, like parents, weren't supposed to have favorites, and really, he didn't, but Jessie was always refreshing with her determined attitude. He was glad that she was here, especially after his emotional first appointment with Mrs. Burnett.

"Hey, Dr. Park. Did you bring this cold air with you?" Jessie grinned as he walked into the exam room. A thin, white tissue-paper shawl covered her shoulders and breasts. "You could at least see that we get warmer blankets or get someone to turn the heat up in these rooms. It's freezing in here."

Dr. Park grinned back and motioned to the paper gown. "Well, we got our spring fashions out a little early, it seems."

He felt for enlarged glands in her neck and then pulled back the gown to check under her arms before motioning for her to lie down on the exam table.

"No lumps that you've noticed? No unusual aches and pains?" He had learned that urging the patient to talk during the exam of her breasts helped ease whatever embarrassment she might feel, although he knew Jessie was a matter-of-fact sort of person. Like most of the patients he would see today, she wouldn't appreciate small talk, so he stayed with her health conditions. While he was sure she didn't like being examined, she never complained or seemed self-conscious. She likely saw it as just another thing to get through. There were thin, still-pink scars across both of her breasts but no lumps. Her chart had showed that her most recent blood-count workup was good. All good news here.

"I still seem to be more tired that I used to be, but then I don't remember life before all of this that well," Jessie answered, sitting up and casually readjusting the gown to better cover herself.

Dr. Park looked at her chart on the adjacent countertop. "You finished with your weekly chemo . . . when? Looks like three weeks ago?"

"Yep," Jessie answered with a grin.

Dr. Park closed the file, giving Jessie a reassuring smile. "Well, it's not uncommon for the fatigue from chemo to last several years."

Years? That wasn't what she wanted to hear. She had hoped that he might put her on some iron supplements or suggest something—anything—to give her more energy.

"It's not uncommon, no, but let's see how you feel in three months. Are you exercising? Getting enough rest? Everything checks out great. It just takes some time to regain stamina. You'll get there."

Jessie didn't hear any of that, except for the phrase "three months."

"I don't have to see you for three months?" she asked, a smile lighting up her entire face.

"Seems about right," Dr. Park said, matching her smile with one of his own. "Sound okay to you?"

Jessie couldn't stop the smile from growing. "Okay? It sounds fabulous. Three months! Oh, my gosh. That's terrific."

"You're doing great," Dr. Park repeated, and Jessie knew her fifteen minutes were up. She thanked him as he closed her chart, told her he'd see her then, and quietly closed the door. Jessie joyfully stuffed the paper gown into the trash container and quickly dressed, eager to share the news she hadn't even realized she'd been waiting to hear.

As she walked down the hallway to the green room, she stole glances into the other consultation rooms. Karen sat in a side chair in one, flipping through a magazine and didn't notice Jessie as she walked past. In the next room sat Marcie, staring out the window, apparently lost in thought. She didn't see Pam in any of the rooms and was relieved. She shouldn't be here. Maybe she'd been there earlier, though. Jessie hoped not but couldn't shake the worry that had formed the last time they'd seen each other. Pam had seemed upset over something. Hopefully, it didn't involve her health.

Jessie said a silent prayer that her friends would all receive good reports today.

She wondered what had happened to Irene. She hadn't seen her for almost a month, not since her last three-hour treatment. In fact, she hadn't seen her since the day they had all laughed at Karen's comment about her sausage fingers and Marcie's addition on moon-pie faces. She remembered how the mask Irene always wore over her nose and mouth had quivered, giving away the fact that the conversation had made her laugh.

Irene never entered their conversations, but Jessie knew she wasn't alone in feeling as if the older woman was part of the group. It wasn't uncommon for the women to get on different treatment schedules for a few days, and Jessie thought that was probably what had happened. She hoped so. Jessie last knew that Irene's blood count had been off.

She was probably getting treatments on a different day. Still, it seemed odd that she wasn't here today. Dr. Park only came once a month.

Jessie couldn't stop from smiling to herself as she walked down the corridor. It was a strange and wonderful feeling to know her days in the treatment center were drawing to an end. The green room had been a huge part of her life for what had seemed like an eternity. She would still have a treatment every third Thursday of the month, but it would be a short one. Maybe an hour at most, the nurse had told her. She wouldn't miss the long hours sitting in the black recliner, but the memory of those days wasn't as horrific as she'd thought it would be. There had been tender moments, laughter, a connection on a level she couldn't have imagined only months ago. Sharing life with another was a blessing, but the idea that you might also be sharing death . . . well, maybe that was a blessing too.

She stopped by the nurses' station to let them know she was finished with the appointment and to see if they needed anything from her, although she couldn't imagine what that might be. They had her entire life history in the file.

"Hey, guys," she said with a genuine smile. The center's director and the two nurses who administered the chemo drugs, took their vital signs, and gave the dreaded booster shot each week had become something like family. They certainly knew more about her and her body than she knew about each of them, but still she felt a closeness to them.

"New pictures?" she asked Susan, the director, motioning to the framed photographs of an infant. She remembered at her last chemo treatment overhearing the staff talk about the expected arrival of a new grandbaby.

Susan smiled, turning the frames toward Jessie. "My baby had a baby. Can't believe it. He's a real charmer. How are you? We won't be seeing much of you, I understand. An hour a month? And you won't see Dr. Park for a while either, I hear. That's great!"

Jessie smiled back, understanding the comment that would likely sound pretty strange in other circumstances. "Not for three months! I was hoping Dr. Park would say so long, but I guess he just likes seeing me."

The staff laughed, and Jessie joined in. It felt good, unconstrained. Different from the cautious laughter over the course of the past few months.

"I like your hair," one of the nurses said. "I didn't realize you were wearing a wig all those weeks until Susan told me. It was really cute, but so is your hair, and I'll bet it feels a whole lot better."

Jessie admitted that it did. "Wigs are great, but hair is better," she said.

After exclaiming again about the darling addition to Susan's family, she said her good-byes, anxious to leave the center.

She suddenly remembered a moment from several weeks ago, when Irene's hand had come out from under the white blanket to reach for the most recent photos Marcie was sharing of her children. She had simply smoothed a finger over the faces of the children and then had silently handed the photos back to Marcie.

The action had stunned the other women. And made them wonder if there had been or still were children in

Irene's life. They hadn't asked. The timing hadn't seemed right.

Jessie turned back to the window to share the memory with the staff now and watched as their faces changed. "So how is Irene?" she asked, her voice dropping to a mere whisper. Suddenly, she already knew the answer, but some part of her heart and head needed to hear it.

Susan glanced down and then raised her eyes to meet Jessie's questioning look. She silently shook her head. "A couple of weeks ago," she said, answering Jessie's next question before she could ask. "Her cancer was pretty advanced when it was discovered. She knew that. We miss her. But she gave it a good fight."

Jessie simply nodded, appreciating Susan's tenderness and her understanding that Jessie needed to accept that Irene's situation had been entirely different from her own. She touched Susan's hand and turned to leave. It felt like she'd been sucker-punched. Jessie had grown to hate that term, "a good fight." People seemed to use it only in reference to fighting cancer, which was an unfair fight in the best of circumstances. A good fight. Although she hated the phrase, she understood the sentiment. She'd put up a good fight herself. And she was doing okay—great. Dr. Park had said so just minutes ago. Irene had put up a good fight, but she had lost. Jessie didn't know the circumstances of what her friend had faced or at what point she had entered the "fight." But she felt such a blow. After all, they had been in the ring together.

Chapter 39

The good news Jessie had received after her checkup was tempered by the sorrow she felt in hearing about Irene. She hadn't known Irene, not really, but the older woman had been a steady presence in Jessie's life for months, and her loss—any loss—seemed to reflect upon them all. It was a cruel reminder that this disease was a killer. Could be a killer. It wasn't always. Jessie's mind was in turmoil. She fought to remember Dr. Park's good news for her: no more examinations for three months!

Jessie walked through the treatment room, noticing a woman she had never seen before. The woman was signing the countless pages of documents required to begin chemo. A man seated beside her was listening intently to the nurse, with a shocked but resigned look.

After pushing open the heavy door to the center, Jessie was crossing the parking lot when a hand suddenly caught the sleeve of her pullover. Jessie gasped.

Karen laughed at Jessie's alarm. "I called your name several times. You're really lost in thought," she said. "Sorry to scare you. How was your report?"

Jessie smiled in relief, working her mind to refocus on the good news. "Hi, Karen. Good checkup! No more appointments for three months. Three months! I'm thrilled. I'll be glad when I'm done altogether, but I'm getting closer. How about you?" She figured from the smile on Karen's face that Dr. Park had given her a good report, too.

"Great! Blood work came back clear. He didn't feel any lumps, and the lymph glands are good," she answered. "I still have radiation ahead of me, but that's just a precaution, he says. I'm not looking forward to it, but it beats more chemo, for sure. I had dreaded taking that much time off work, but I resigned last week, so that's not an issue."

Jessie was surprised. "You resigned? Really? I know you liked working."

"I did. I do. I'll look for something different after the six weeks of radiation." Karen looked good, more relaxed than Jessie had seen her. "You know, I think it was the best thing. They were going to keep me on at work but only to be nice, and because, legally, they pretty much had to, I think. But I'm ready for something new. I'm actually excited about it."

Both women turned as the door to the treatment center opened. Marcie walked across the gravel parking lot to join them. Jessie realized this was the only time they'd visited outside of the center. She was enjoying it, and her sorrow upon learning of Irene's passing was soothed by the good news her friends were sharing.

"You're smiling," Karen said, making Marcie smile even brighter.

She looked so young in her ball cap and sneakers. Jessie suddenly felt protective of her against Karen's abruptness—she spoke so often without thinking.

"I *am* smiling," Marcie replied. "Good report. Wonderful report. The second MRI and additional biopsy showed that what Dr. Park thought might be another lump was only scar tissue. Thank God! I don't know if I could have gone through all of this again."

Rather than being pleased, Karen was appalled. "You mean he put you through all of that and scared you half to death for nothing? Good grief."

Marcie seemed to take it in stride. They all had a good understanding of Karen and her glass-half-empty attitude after all of their months together. Karen was just Karen, and that was okay. People weren't perfect. Karen's tirades were, for the most part, because she wasn't sure of what else to say. She didn't mean any harm.

Marcie couldn't stop smiling. "Well, it was worth it. I'm glad we didn't wait to have it checked out. Marc actually wanted to change oncologists; that's how upset he was. I'm just glad all the waiting is over. Sometimes I think waiting to find out test results is the worst part of all of this."

"Oh, I don't know about that," Karen answered, shaking her head.

Marcie and Jessie grinned at each other.

"I'll bet Marc is beside himself with relief," Jessie said, trying to keep the conversation on a positive track. She hadn't been particularly impressed with Marcie's good-looking husband, but at least he seemed to have stepped up to the plate in the last few weeks. He'd stopped by the green room several times to take Marcie to lunch after treatments, and he was always polite to the rest of them, if a little reserved. Jessie had noticed that Marcie had seemed a little reserved herself whenever Marc showed up. She didn't know anything about their marriage—Marcie primarily talked about their children—but she hoped the relationship was good. A diagnosis of cancer could strengthen a relationship or deepen chasms that were already there. She hoped, for Marcie's sake, that everything was going well at home. She certainly seemed good this morning, with the threat of more surgeries, treatments, and uncertainty removed. Actually, she seemed great, if not particularly eager to talk about her husband.

"I'm going to run downtown and buy something. I don't know what but *something*," Marcie said, laughing at herself as much as to her friends. "Anybody up for joining me?"

The invitation took both Karen and Jessie by surprise. The women had never done anything together outside of the green room. The idea of taking the friendship to a different level was a little daunting. Would they have anything in common, other than cancer?

"I really have to get home," Karen said, "but have fun. Buy something extravagant. You deserve it." She said her good-byes and walked across the parking lot to her car, waving as she got in.

Jessie was torn between accepting Marcie's offer and just going home herself. She was anxious to let Greg know that everything was good after her exam. Better than good; it felt like the end to a prison term. "Another time," she answered, smiling at the younger woman and meaning the words. "I'm wondering about Pam. Have you seen her or talked to her? I'm kind of worried about her. I saw her briefly after my last chemo and asked why she was here, but she didn't answer; she just changed the subject."

Marcie shook her head. "I think that's the last time I saw her. We didn't really visit. I was getting a treatment, and she was talking with the staff. Do you have her phone number?"

"I do," Jessie answered, "though I've never called her."

"Let me know if you hear anything from her," Marcie said and moved toward her own vehicle. "A good day for both of us, huh? Enjoy the rest of it."

Jessie slid into her own car and rummaged through her purse for the slip of paper with Pam's phone number on it. She knew exactly where it was. She'd seen it several times over the course of her treatments as she'd changed purses with the seasons. She had clung to it like a lifeline, always knowing it was there, just as she always knew Pam was there, if she needed her. What if her friend had needed her, and she'd never made the same offer? She fought the urge to wait until she got home to make the call, knowing she might not call if she did. She pulled out her cell phone and tapped in the number.

She listened to the ringing phone as she watched people come and go from the hospital's back entrance. Only staff, easily recognized by their different colors of scrubs, seemed to be happy. *Probably headed to lunch*, Jessie thought, *or maybe even getting off work*. Everyone else walked with purpose toward their vehicles, heads down.

Pam answered on the fourth ring, sounding slightly breathless. Jessie was suddenly nervous and afraid that something was terribly wrong. What reason would her friend have to be in the green room unless that was the case?

"Pam, hi. It's Jessie. Jessie Gifford." She knew she sounded nervous. She was. Maybe instead of being a good friend she was just being nosy.

Typical of Pam, she let Jessie off the hook by taking the lead. "Gee, it's great to hear your voice. I've been thinking about you. You're about finished, aren't you?"

Jessie could hear genuine concern in Pam's voice. "I am," Jessie answered, realizing she *did* have a reason for calling. In her worry about Pam, she'd nearly forgotten her own good news. "Just got through seeing Dr. Park, and all the reports are good."

"Awesome," Pam answered. "What's the schedule like now?"

Jessie was relieved to hear the upbeat note in her friend's voice. "I'll get a different drug once a month—supposedly, it takes about an hour—and I'll see Dr. Park every three months. Three months! I'm ecstatic. I don't know how long that will go on, but it beats every month."

"Probably for a while," Pam replied, "but that's not a big deal. And an hour a month is nothing!"

"Oh, I know. When I think back on the hours and hours in the green room, I'm thrilled to be done with all of that. It feels so good to get to this point. I'm just ready to be completely done, I guess."

Pam didn't immediately answer, and Jessie's concern returned. She was going on about herself and how great she was doing, but that wasn't why she had called.

"How are you?" Jessie asked quietly, afraid to hear the answer. "I've been thinking about you since I saw you in the center. You seemed kind of down that day, and we didn't have time to talk. Pam, is everything okay?" In the background, she could hear ice cubes being dropped into a glass and the sounds of items being moved around. She wondered if Pam was on the patio that she talked about so often. That was something they had in common. Both relished the moments of solitude they could find outdoors. "On your patio?" Jessie asked. "I can hear you fixing a drink."

Pam laughed. "Well, it's only iced tea, which I seem to be addicted to, and yes, I'm on *a* patio, just not my old one. I sold the house and moved to a much smaller place—a condo, actually—but it's starting to feel like home."

"Wow, that's big news," Jessie said. "You mentioned you were planning to move." She wondered if that was why Pam seemed to be down the last time she'd seen her. Could be. She knew the house was where Pam had lived with her late husband. She had finally shared that aspect of her life with the other women. Selling it had to have been difficult.

"What prompted you to do that?" Jessie asked. As soon as the words were out of her mouth, she dreaded hearing the answer.

"Oh, it was just time," Pam replied. "Past time, really. All of Stephen's clothes were still hanging in the closets. His toiletries were still where he'd left them. I knew I was clinging to the past. I guess it took a nudge to make me move forward."

"So what was the nudge? Pam, is everything okay?" Jessie could almost feel Pam's hesitation.

"Honestly? I couldn't afford to keep the house," Pam said. "It was larger than I needed anyway. It was the right time, and, amazingly, I feel so much lighter in the condo, less burdened. And it's been fun to fix up, to make it mine."

"And you're doing okay? Health-wise?" She could hear Pam taking a drink of tea and then setting the glass down. Jessie knew she was hedging her answer. What was wrong? Was the cancer back? After all this time? She knew it could happen. She had read articles and had watched talk shows about women who were two-time or even three-time breast cancer survivors. Jessie didn't want to hear that was what was happening with her friend, both for Pam's sake and, selfishly, for her own.

Even though she hadn't talked with Pam much or seen her for weeks, she held her friend up to the level she herself hoped to reach. Pam was finished with all of this. Jessie was close. She didn't want to have the floor fall out from under either one of them. Not now.

"I'm good, Jessie," she answered. Her tone had gone serious. "I really am. No lumps. Blood work all good. I just didn't know if you had heard."

"Heard what?" Jessie could feel her own heart pounding.

"Well, I had stopped into the center that day to see if I could donate some blankets," Pam explained. "I had a whole closet full of nice ones, and those thin white sheets they call blankets are a sad excuse for giving warmth to anyone going through chemo. They were happy to take them. That's when I heard about Irene. I just couldn't believe it. I knew she wasn't doing well and had been in and out of the hospital, but still . . . I guess I thought she'd make it."

Jessie realized she'd been holding her breath and quietly exhaled. "I just heard this morning. Damn, it makes me so sad. I was surprised, too."

She knew they were both more than just surprised. To hear that someone had died from a disease that you have—*had*—is a hard jolt of reality, a truth they worked hard to keep in the background as they went on about life. They would all miss Irene and remember her. Always.

The phone line was silent, both of the women lost in thought and remembrance.

"So you're okay?" Jessie asked again.

"I am," Pam answered, the lift returning to her voice. "Everything is good, health-wise. Emotionally, too. It's been an adjustment to live in a different place is all. A place I had never shared with Stephen, but it's good. I was ready for change."

They ended the conversation with both saying they should get together soon. Jessie thought maybe they really would now. Just talking about something other than their health seemed to have moved their friendship to a new level. She made a mental note to see if Pam could meet for lunch soon and then realized that she hadn't eaten yet today, and her stomach growled at the acknowledgement.

Chapter 40

Marcie flipped through the rack of colorful spring tops at the department store. The mix of colors surprised and delighted her. The brightness fit her mood. This had been a great day. An amazing, fabulous day! The relief she felt at learning the "suspicious" lump was only scar tissue was indescribable. She felt like a superhero, as if nothing in the world was impossible. If she wanted to fly, she thought she probably could.

She couldn't remember the last time she had been so filled with joy or the last time she'd gone shopping for herself. By herself. With no kids in tow. They wouldn't be out of school for hours; Marc was working out of town today. This day was hers! It would have been fun if Jessie and Karen could have joined her. Maybe. Or they all could have felt awkward with each other outside of the green room. She didn't really believe that, though. Jessie would have made it fun. But wow, this was fun, too. She was enjoying the freedom. She needed to do this more often.

"Just looking," she replied with a smile when the salesclerk asked if she needed help. As the young woman walked away, Marcie caught a whiff of her perfume and paused.

Was that the same scent she had discovered on Marc's shirt? It sure seemed the same. Strong. Musky. The girl had to be in her early twenties, at best. She was wearing way too much perfume, for sure. It lingered in the air, even after the girl had left, and Marcie had a fleeting thought that she really shouldn't wear such a strong fragrance at work. Did her employer approve? The clothes were likely to pick up the scent.

Is that what had happened? Had Marc simply been around some woman wearing too much perfume? Maybe even this girl? She paused with her hand on one of the racks and tried to remember how his shirt had smelled, where it had smelled. The collar? The sleeve? She had tossed it into the laundry that day along with other shirts and had tried to put it out of her thoughts. Except that she hadn't. There were just too many issues on her mind at the time, and she hadn't wanted to deal with this one. Especially this one.

Marc had never been unfaithful in their twelve years of marriage. Not that she knew of, anyway. *And where did that thought originate?* She had never even suspected him of cheating, not until she had smelled that shirt. What was wrong with her? Why was she thinking like this? Were her thoughts less steady because of all she'd been through in the past months or more steady because of it? She had the beginnings of a headache.

What had Dr. Park told her? "Let's deal with what we know, not what we can imagine." *Easy for him to say*, Marcie now thought with a wry smile. It wasn't his body; it wasn't his life. It wasn't his marriage.

And what *did* she know for a fact? That a shirt Marc had dropped into the hamper weeks ago had smelled of perfume. She also knew he had stepped up in the last month or so, helping more with the kids, chipping in with tasks around the house, and being especially attentive toward her.

"Wow, such horrible problems," Marcie said to herself, realizing that the thought sounded like something Jessie would say. Apparently, her green-room friend's attitude had rubbed off on her. Why borrow trouble? Especially now, when she was seeing an end to this long, dark nightmare.

Marcie decided that her friend was right. Jessie always seemed to be optimistic. Maybe it was because her stars were in alignment. The idea made Marcie laugh. Jessie had told all of them about her stars and that whenever she saw them, she just had a calming feeling that everything was going to be okay. *"It works because I believe it works,"* she had told them, suggesting they should try it. And she had been absolutely serious about it.

Maybe it really is that simple, Marcie thought. She had the power to let this shirt thing go. If something was going on with Marc and if she did find proof of it, she'd deal with it then. She wasn't going to stress over what she could imagine. Good grief, she could imagine much more than a smelly shirt in the hamper if she really wanted to go with what could be. She'd go with what she knew to be true. For herself, not for Marc.

Right now, she wanted something new and colorful and young to wear. It was a good day—a fabulous day—and she wasn't going to let anything ruin it. Her imagination could just take a break. Enough already. Of all the side effects she had gone through with cancer and chemo, the best was the strength she had gained. Whatever came in the future, she could handle it. Maybe it was true; she'd become a superhero.

She spotted a loose-fitting, green-striped linen shirt and knew it was perfect. It would go with everything and looked super comfortable—a trend in selecting clothes over the past few months that would likely take a while to break. Plus, she would need comfortable tops for awhile yet.

Now that the fear with the scar tissue had been eliminated, she had to face having breast reconstruction surgery. That meant more hospitals, more doctor appointments, more discomfort, but she could deal with all of that. As Dr. Park had explained, the reconstruction of her body was a positive thing, a step on the healing side of this cancer equation.

She could think about the future now. As the thought settled into her mind, she realized she'd been holding her breath all these weeks, unable to think or plan beyond the next doctor's appointment, the next medical test. All of her energy had gone toward summoning up the strength to deal with whatever came next. It was time—past time—to turn some of that energy toward her own happiness, her own future. Maybe go back to work. Or back to school. At the very least, go back to spending time with her girlfriends. A night out with silly laughter and a drink stronger than herbal tea was definitely in order.

As she carried the colorful shopping bag with the name of the store embossed on the side and her new shirt inside,

Marcie realized she was smiling with joy, an emotion she hadn't noticed was missing from her life until it was back. She was making a conscious decision to be happy. It felt good.

Chapter 41

Karen dropped her car keys and purse on the kitchen counter and noticed the blinking light on their answering machine. "Jon?" she called. No reply. Looking out the sliding patio doors, she could see him bent over the tomato plants they'd bought over the weekend. It was way too early to put them in the ground, but the tiny plants were already covered in blooms, so if they didn't get a late freeze, they might be fine. At the least, Jon would enjoy fussing over them.

Smiling to herself, she hit the button on the machine to hear any messages that might have been left.

"Karen?" The woman's voice didn't sound familiar, and for a split second, Karen felt panic that it was a nurse at any number of doctors' offices. But she'd just left the oncologist. All was good, so that couldn't be it. Could it?

She was nearly holding her breath as the message played.

"This is Teresa Miller, human resources director at MSR Industries. We reviewed your résumé and job application, and, if you are still interested, we'd very much like to visit with you."

If she was still interested? They'd like to visit with her? She'd like that very much. Very, very much. *Oh, my God*, she thought. *Someone wants me.*

This day was getting better and better. She wasn't sure it could get any better, which was an unfamiliar and strange feeling for her. She was quite aware of what everyone else knew—she wasn't a very optimistic person. But she was trying. The women she had met in the green room had helped her with that. *Everything is relative*, she thought, grinning.

She had gotten a great report from Dr. Park. Two friends had also gotten great reports. A cute, young woman had invited her to go shopping. And now, the prospect of a new job!

Would they want her if they knew she was completing chemo for breast cancer? Or that she'd still have to have some time off for checkups and blood work?

Fatigue was still an issue, but perhaps going back to work would be just what she needed to gain new energy. She would meet new people, have responsibilities, and best of all, she would have a reason for getting up every morning.

She was getting ahead of herself, she knew. The message just said they wanted to interview her for the job. She didn't have the job. Yet. But she'd get it, she told herself, unable to stop smiling. Oh, yes, she would!

She was thrilled, and she knew Jon would be over the top. He had enjoyed having her around more, but he also knew she was a happier person when she was working and had other people in her life to fret about.

She fixed herself a glass of soda (it finally tasted good again) and slid open the patio door. First, she had to tell Jon that her report from the oncologist had been good, that her friends had had good reports too, and that she had a solid lead on a job. Then she would tell him that he'd placed the tomato plants too close together.

Chapter 42

Jessie still sat in her car in the parking lot behind the treatment center. She had sent Greg a text message from her phone, letting him know the appointment had gone great. "Done for three months!" she had typed. He hadn't answered yet. He might not, if he was busy at work. That was okay. She was happy on her own. The coffee she had stopped to buy at the convenience store on her way to the appointment was cold now, but it still tasted good.

She leaned back against the seat and took a long breath. She felt relaxed, perhaps for the first time in months. And optimistic. The future was back, and she relished the new feeling that anything was possible. She hadn't realized that the thought was gone until now, until it returned.

All of the women from the green room had been just existing, making it through each day, day by day. Waiting to find out if the surgeries, the treatments, and the drugs would work; if they could wonder about the future; if it was okay to make plans and to follow dreams.

She hoped Marcie was having a great time shopping and that she'd found something to buy that she couldn't wait to wear. That was always such a fun feeling. She'd never seen her friend in anything other than sweatpants or jeans.

With three young kids, that was probably pretty much her uniform every day. Even so, she was such a cutie with her ball caps and pro football jerseys. Jessie was relieved and happy that her young friend's latest scare had proven to be only that. She knew from personal experience how much mental work it took to let the fear go. She hoped Marcie had been able to do that and had enjoyed her day.

She jumped as her cell phone beeped, letting her know a text message had arrived and then grinned at Greg's one word reply to her news: "YES!"

Sipping her coffee, she thought of Pam and was glad she had called her. Thank heavens her health was okay. Selfishly, Jessie knew that if the cancer had returned for Pam, it would be a blow for all of them. She would have been ashamed of the thought, but she knew it was something they all understood.

It had to be difficult too for Pam to accept that Irene was gone. She was closer to her than any of the other women; they had gone through chemo together.

Pam had sounded enthusiastic about the sale of her home and about moving. Still, Jessie imagined that had to be hard.

Even Karen had seemed happier this morning than Jessie had ever seen her. The thought made her smile. She'd come to enjoy the other woman's wry comments and challenging attitude. Everyone needed a Karen in her life.

Jessie wasn't sure why she was lingering in the parking lot. True, there wasn't anything she needed to do or anywhere she needed to be, but she sure didn't want or need to be *here.* She pulled the seatbelt on, turned the key, and put the car in reverse. Out of the blue, she thought of the woman she had just seen in the green room, a woman starting her own long journey today—the day when Jessie and her three friends were close enough to the end to feel hope and a sense of finally being cut loose from the bindings of treatment.

Her mind went to Irene, and she said a prayer that she was at peace and finally out of pain, and she made a promise to remember her.

Suddenly, she pulled her vehicle back into the parking spot, unclipped her seatbelt, and made her way back into the center.

The nurses behind the glass window looked up in surprise as she came through the door. They smiled at her with a questioning look. Another nurse sat on the armless metal stool, a plastic binder full of forms in front of her.

Barbara Burnett, white-faced and obviously frightened, sat erect in one of the black vinyl recliners, her eyes huge as she listened to the nurse and signed here, and here, and here, as her husband looked on.

Jessie took a seat in the adjacent recliner. The nurse looked knowingly up at her and then back to her new patient.

Barbara looked up at Jessie, tears filling her eyes.

Smiling gently at the woman, Jessie put a hand on her arm. "Your first day; almost my last. Looking back, it seems like it has gone quickly, but I know it doesn't feel that way to you right now. I heard the nurse call you Barbara. My name is Jessie, by the way."

Then Jessie added in a quiet voice, "I've been where you are. It's a little overwhelming, isn't it?"

Acknowledgments

Thank you, first and foremost, dear readers, for proving that people *will* read a book about women taking the walk through breast cancer.

I hope the stories of these five women will give inspiration, strength, and—hopefully—a laugh or two to those facing that challenge themselves and enlighten those who know someone taking the hard walk.

Don't forget to roar occasionally. It truly does help.

This book would not have been written without the constant support and encouragement of my family, even when it took much longer than I said it would. I love you all.

The input and talents of my earliest readers, critics, editors, and friends, Lynne Thompson Guillory and Eileen Robertson, made my writing so much better. I hope you both know how much you mean to me.

And thank you to everyone at Mill City Press and Hillcrest Media for taking my pages and turning them into a beautiful book.

About the Author

A native of Kansas, Jackie Ryan Witherspoon holds degrees in writing from both Kansas State University and the University of Kansas. She published a newspaper and then a magazine before turning to fiction. Her writing also has appeared in numerous regional and national magazines.

Jackie enjoys writing emotional and compelling books about strong women, drawing inspiration from true stories.

She now writes full time from her home on Table Rock Lake in Missouri, where she lives with her husband, Gary, and a yellow lab, Katie, who naps beside her desk, offering encouragement and companionship and forcing much-needed breaks.

Visit the author online at
www.jackieryanwitherspoon.com.